THE CHALLENGE

"You will take *me*. Perhaps with your . . . skill, you can find the land of water."

"I don't think so," I said uncertainly. If I was lucky, with my skill I could hear footsteps coming, I could guess where to look for a sticky needle, but what Gray Fire was asking was too much. I was not ready. Not quite.

"Say yes," Gray Fire urged. "Say yes." No one had ever made a request of me with such need in his voice. It made me feel scared and important at the same time. *Sometimes,* the weroance had said when she gave me my name, *the people need someone to do the impossible. . . . Someone with the ability to see what can't be seen. . . .*

"I'll try."

Printed in the United States of America.

This book is set in 14 1/2-point Perpetua.
Designed by Mara Van Fleet.

Library of Congress Cataloging-in-Publication Data
Dorris, Michael
Sees Behind Trees / Michael Dorris—1st ed.
p.   cm
Summary: A Native American boy with a special gift to "see" beyond his poor
eyesight journeys with an old warrior to a land of mystery and beauty.
ISBN 0-7868-1290-7
1. Indians of North America—Juvenile fiction. [1. Indians of North America—
Fiction. 2. Blind—Fiction. 3. Physically handicapped—Fiction] I. Title.
PZ7.D7287Sj 1996
[Fic]—dc20
96-15859

Portions of this book, in slightly altered form, have appeared in *Disney Adventures* magazine
and *Aboriginal Voices* magazine.

Other books by the same author

➜

Fiction for young readers
Morning Girl
Guests

Adult fiction
A Yellow Raft in Blue Water
The Crown of Columbus (with Louise Erdrich)
Working Men
Cloud Chamber

Adult nonfiction
The Broken Cord
Paper Trail
Rooms in the House of Stone

For Persia, who teaches me how to sing
For Pallas, who teaches me how to laugh
For Aza, who teaches me how to dance
For Louise, who teaches me how to listen

SEES
BEHIND
TREES

→

MICHAEL
DORRIS

HYPERION PAPERBACKS FOR CHILDREN

New York

This book would not be but for the careful, intelligent editorial guidance of Elizabeth Gordon, and for the ideas, encouragements, critiques, and patience of Louise Erdrich. My special thanks go also to Sandi Campbell, Lisa Holton, Donna Bray, Charles Rembar, Lauren Wohl, Ellen Friedman, and Suzanne Harper. I am indebted to the work of Helen C. Rountree and recommend her study *The Powhatan Indians of Virginia* (University of Oklahoma Press, 1989) to all who wish to learn more about the peoples imagined in these pages.

CHAPTER 1

"TRY HARDER. TRACK IT with your eye before you shoot."

My mother's anxious voice snapped in my ear as loudly as the string of my bow.

"Track what?" I asked for the third time this morning. Before me all I could see was the familiar blur of green and brown that meant I was outside in the forest on a sunny day. Then, by squinting, I could sense something coming toward me, smell the familiar pemmican scent of berries mixed with dried meat, recognize the tread of moccasins I had heard a thousand times before. Gradually one blurry image began to stand out from all the others and an instant later it turned into my approaching mother. When she was close enough for me to touch, I could tell from her face and from the tenseness of her body that she was worried.

"This," she said, shaking the clump of moss that she held in one hand. In the other were the four arrows I had already shot, which she dropped at my feet. "When I throw the moss in the air, imagine its flight and then aim where you think it will be by the time your arrow meets it. It's not so hard, and every boy must learn how to do it before he can become a man."

A rumbling noise came from my stomach and my mother smiled her I've-got-an-idea smile. "Think of the moss as your breakfast," she suggested. "Imagine it is a corn cake, hot from the ashes, soooo delicious."

I could almost taste it on my tongue, feel its crunch as I bit down, smell the sweet fullness it would bring. "Couldn't I eat first, just this once?" I pleaded. "I'm sure I could find the moss in the sky if I weren't so hungry."

For a moment I thought my mother would give in, and I leaned toward her, blinking as though a steaming golden corn cake would appear in her hand to replace the straggly plant. But all that changed was my mother's expression.

"Walnut." My name in her mouth was tired, pounded into flour. "You know the rule: you must find the target before breakfast can find you."

I nodded. If that was the rule, I wouldn't eat for a long time. We had faced this matter of what I couldn't see many times before—when my mother would point to something I couldn't locate or throw a ball I couldn't catch—but it had never before been such serious business. Now we couldn't just act as though nothing was wrong. Now we had to solve the problem. We had struggled with it every morning since, three days ago, my mother had decided it was time to teach me, her oldest child, how to use a bow and arrow. I had never once succeeded and I knew that sooner or later she would give up, make some excuse, and feed me. But it would not be soon.

"Maybe if you made your eyes smaller?" My mother encouraged me by bringing her cheeks so close to her forehead that she looked like a dried onion, and I made the mistake of laughing.

"Today . . . ," my mother said in the same voice she had used when I was younger and she told me not to play with sharp knives. She picked up an arrow from the ground and sternly held it out for me to take. She walked back toward the place where she threw the moss into the air. "Today, we will *not* surrender." Before I could object she had disappeared again into that mist of color and noise that surrounded me like the roof and walls of a very small house.

"Now!"

I quickly pointed my arrow high above the place where her voice came from, and released it.

"Better," she called. "The sunlight must have confused you. Try again."

→   ←

There were many *other* things I could do, I told myself when finally, with not a single victory, we came home. I could make a whistle from a stiff reed using only the sharp edge of a clamshell. I could sing a song after hearing it just one time. I could find wild strawberries, even clusters of violets, by closing my eyes and following the directions of my nose. I could hear my father's footsteps before anyone else. "He's back," I would inform my brothers and sisters, giving them a little longer to stop playing and compose themselves. So why couldn't I shoot?

"Is there some trick to it?" I asked my mother's brother, Brings the Deer, one evening as we were sitting in front of our house, watching fireflies as they flickered before our faces. He was the best archer in our whole family, so he should know.

"Practice is the only trick," my uncle said, sounding more like my father than himself. Usually, since he was younger than my mother and didn't yet have any children of his own, he was less serious.

"It's been days and days, and I'm no better."

"Maybe . . ." Brings the Deer's tone was gentler, more understanding. "Maybe your bowstring is not tight enough?" He reached over to where it rested by my leg and tested it. "No, it seems all right. Maybe you're closing your eyes at the last moment before you shoot? *I* did that myself when I first started."

I shook my head.

"Maybe . . . How many fingers am I holding up?"

I tipped my head. The dusky light was dim, but I could still see my own hands, balled into fists. "Fingers?"

"How many?"

I couldn't tell how many arms he was holding up, much less fingers. "Three?" I guessed.

"How many now?"

"Two?"

"Now?"

"Five?"

There was a silence. "Walnut, I was holding up no fingers at all."

"I knew that," I said, though it wasn't true. "I was making a joke."

But Brings the Deer didn't laugh.

The next morning when my mother woke me for shooting practice, we went to a new part of the forest. That was only the first odd thing.

"Put down your bow and sit on this rock," my mother said, patting a large flat stone at the base of a pine tree. Then, from her sack she brought out a tightly woven sash, placed it over my eyes, and tied it with a length of grapevine.

"What are you doing?" I wanted to know.

"Shhh," she said. "Describe this place to me."

"But I've never been here before and I can't see."

"Shhh," she said again. "Look with your ears."

At first, there was nothing to hear—just . . . for-

5

est. But the longer we didn't talk, the more separate parts announced themselves: the hush of a brook just behind me and, farther beyond that, the rush of a river. The buzz of a beehive on a tree not far over to my right. The beat of a hummingbird's wings as it dove in and out of a cluster of . . . what was that smell? . . . *roses* near where my mother—who, I could tell, had just oiled her hair this morning—sat.

"Don't move," I said as I heard her prepare to shift her weight. "It's only a hummingbird."

"*What's* only a . . . ? Oh," she whispered. "How beautiful. What else do you see, Walnut?"

So I told her—there were so many things that it took the whole morning to list them all. And the amazing fact was, I completely forgot to be hungry for breakfast. From that day on, instead of shooting arrows we went each dawn to a new spot and stayed until I had surprised my mother at least four times by what I could see but she could not.

At the end of the summer there was always a great feast—and that was when boys my age had to prove by their accurate shooting that they were ready to be grown up.

"I'm not going," I told Brings the Deer. We were lying on our backs on the bank of the pond at the south end of the village, waiting for fish to swim into our net. "You said I had to practice and I have not practiced. Instead I played games with my mother."

"So she's told me," he said. All around us was the noise of people working. Some were gathering hollow green and yellow gourds in huge piles that made a popping sound when they knocked together. Others were stacking firewood—I could hear them stumbling up with their arms full, dropping the load with a rolling crash, and then the even tap-tap-tap of setting the logs straight. Even Brings the Deer was replacing the old bluebird feathers on his fancy headband with new ones. From off to one side I picked up the rich hickory smell of stewing venison.

"My father will be ashamed." My best friend Frog was, I knew, even now out somewhere practicing his aim. I didn't know why he was nervous—he told me that he had been able to shoot moss out of the air on his very first try.

"Have you asked him?"

"Who, Frog?" Had even Brings the Deer heard of Frog's talent?

"Your father. Have you talked to him about this?"

"No, but . . . he's coming now."

Brings the Deer stood up and looked all around. "Where?"

"On the other side of the pond," I told him, just as my father called our names.

"Walnut? Brings the Deer? Where are you?"

"I see him now," said my uncle. "Over here," he yelled.

While we waited for my father—he walked like a

beaver, his feet flat and wide apart—to make his way over to us, Brings the Deer sat next to me and shook his head. "It's amazing," he laughed, and admired the design of the new feathers. "My sister did not exaggerate."

Before I could say anything, my father burst from the rest of the colors around us and sat down on my stomach.

"Ah," he sighed, and stretched his arms. "A dry, comfortable seat at last."

"I can't breathe!" I tried to shove him off me, but he was too heavy.

"How very strange," my father said to Brings the Deer. "I thought I heard my son speak from inside my own body."

"Yes," Brings the Deer replied. "It's what a bird must feel when she sits on her nest after the chicks hatch."

"I am sinking into the mud," I muttered, and poked my father beneath his ribs with my finger. Why was he being so playful, as if I were still a very little boy?

"What's this? What's this?" he cried, cocking his head and jumping up. "Walnut, what are you doing down there? Come home quickly. The contests are going to start early."

"Father . . . ," I began. How I hated to embarrass him.

"No time for talking. This year there is going to be an extra trial, *much* harder."

"Harder than hitting a target?" I might as well stay

in the mud instead of cleaning up.

Boys my age were already waiting in the clearing where ball games were played. Each one had his bow and quiver of arrows. As we passed my friend Frog close enough for me to glance directly into his face I realized that though he was nervous and excited, he wasn't half as unhappy as I felt. The flat afternoon sun made the colors of the earth and rocks as bright as if they were wet. There was no wind to stir the branches of the trees and give me an excuse for missing my shots. The sky was the pale, shiny blue of a trout's scale.

Brings the Deer gave my arm a squeeze and then went over to join the crowd of adults and small children watching in the shade nearby. I was sure my mother must be among them. I wondered what she was thinking. When people learned she hadn't taught me how to shoot, they might criticize her. Ay-yah-yah.

The weroance, our most important person, the expert on hunting, stood nearby. She raised her hands for quiet, and when everyone was still, she spoke in the slow, booming voice she saved for the most solemn moments. It seemed to come from deep within her body, to be blown through a horn of shell, to rattle like the skin of a hand drum.

"Sometimes," she said, "the people need someone to do the impossible. As necessary as hunting is, as

necessary as growing and harvesting plants, sometimes we need even more than those tasks can pro-
vide. We need someone with the ability to see what
can't be seen. And we won't have the regular contest
until someone passes this new one."

There was a silence, then all the boys around me
began to whisper to one another.

"What does she mean?" worried one.

"How can they expect us to do that?" another
demanded. "Isn't it enough that our mothers have
taught us how to shoot moss from the sky?"

"So," the weroance went on steady as the beat of a
large bird's wings, "the first test will be for . . ."

I missed what she said because something fell at my
feet. I looked down—it was the sash and a length of
grapevine. My mother must have tossed it.

"See behind *trees*?" Frog repeated the weroance's
words, and the boy next to me looked toward the
forest uncertainly.

But I knew what to do. I tied the sash around my
eyes and remained very still. The wind made fingers
through the trees and I used them to feel my way in
each direction. My mind flew the way a hawk must
fly, skimming over all that was ordinary, alert for a
dart of something out of place. I paid no attention to
the rustle of leaves or the rain of a waterfall. Those
expected sounds—those sounds I knew from all my
morning games with my mother—I put to one side,
and waited.

What was that? A dead branch snapped. A rock, slightly closer, tumbled down a hill. A breath was drawn in.

"Who will begin?" The weroance interrupted my ears. "You," she said.

And Frog tried, without much hope, "I see a raccoon. He is asleep in the bough of a tree."

"You," she said. Another voice, Sleeps Late, no more confident, answered. "I see a . . . spiderweb, strung on the brambles of a mulberry bush."

"Now you," she said, but this time there was no reply. "You. Walnut."

I thought so hard that my head felt tight between my ears. I was afraid to make a mistake in front of so many people, but then I pretended it was my mother asking me to listen, curious and interested as she had been every morning.

"A man is coming from the south," I said. "He is light on his feet but has a limp. He is not young, for he must breathe hard to climb. He is . . ." I stopped talking, shut my eyes even behind my blindfold, and concentrated. There was no mistaking it. "He is laughing! It is Gray Fire!"

I heard people turning to look behind me, whispering among themselves. I could almost *feel* them looking to see if I was right. That part of the forest was dense, the paths overgrown and winding.

"There!" Brings the Deer's voice was loud above the rest. "It is, it *is* Gray Fire!" The weroance's brother! He had been given his name because he was so quiet he could pass through the village like smoke.

Strong hands untied the vine that bound the sash around my eyes. My father's hands. They lingered for just an instant on my hair. I'm sure no one else but me noticed.

"This part of the contest is over," the weroance announced. "Each boy except the one who passed must now prove himself with a bow in order to earn the right to his grown-up name."

"And what of the boy who passed?" my mother called out from where she stood. "What about my Walnut?"

"When a boy passes the test he is no longer a boy," the weroance answered. "He no longer wears a boy's name."

Everyone stopped what they were doing to hear what she would say next. I turned the sash in my hand, the sash my mother had woven. It was soft to the touch, as if it had been made from silky moss.

"Sees Behind Trees," the weroance pronounced, "is now a young man."

CHAPTER 2

I HAD SPENT SO much time worrying about failing the test and not receiving a man's name that I didn't know what to do when I passed it and got one. And I was not alone in my confusion. By the end of the day every boy in the village was someone new—and yet we were also still the same as we had been.

"Remind me," I asked the man who used to be Frog.

"Three Chances," he said in a tone that made me sense his embarrassment.

"There would not have been *enough* chances for me," I reminded him. "We would have still been in the meadow. Maybe I would have had better luck at night. 'No Chance' would have been me."

"How did you do it?" he asked me. "How did you know it was Gray Fire? When I said I saw a raccoon out there I was guessing—though of course I'm sure

13

there *is* a raccoon out there, somewhere."

"My mother taught me how, the same as yours did you with the bow."

"Well, how did *she* do it then? Teach you to see through a sash, to see not just what *could* be in the forest but what actually *was* in the forest?"

I remembered Brings the Deer's advice. "Practice," I said.

Before we could continue, Frog's—I mean Three Chances's—older sister Diver came up to us.

"Wal—, excuse me, Sees Behind Trees," she said. "You've got to help me."

Diver had never spoken directly to me before, much less asked for assistance.

"How?" Suddenly I felt more grown up. Here I was talking to a girl old enough to visit the women's house every month!

"My bone needle," Diver complained. "It took me days and days to shape it, to get the point small enough to follow my awl through deer hide, and to make the eye large enough to welcome sinew without mashing it up. And now it's gone."

"Where did it go?" I tried to sound like my father or Brings the Deer—concerned and sure of myself.

"I lost it," Diver said. "I was sitting by the pond working on a shirt. It was hot—the bugs were biting me—so I jumped in, took a swim. When I got out I couldn't find the needle though I looked for it everywhere."

"She's always doing things like that," Three Chances whispered, but loud enough for Diver to hear him.

"I am not. Only once before."

"What about mother's ladle?"

"That was different," Diver said. "It was old. It just broke."

"It was not meant for prying up cooking rocks."

"*You* should have been doing that work, anyway. But no, as usual you were off playing and I had to do your job as well as mine."

I knew that this sister and brother could talk to each other in this manner for a very long time, so I interrupted.

"I still don't understand," I said to Diver. "Do you want me to help you search for it?"

"No." Her impatience with Frog spilled over and splashed on me. "I want you to *find* it. You know, shut your eyes and see it like you did Gray Fire today."

I was proud that a grown-up girl believed I could do such a thing. I felt more like a man every minute.

"All right," I agreed, and shut my eyes. I listened very hard, listened with every eye of my ear, but all that came to me was the sound of Diver's breathing, the air hissing in and out of her mouth.

"I see a fish," I said, imagining the beat of gills.

Diver's breathing got faster. "Has this fish swallowed my needle?"

"Maybe."

"Maybe?" This was not a word she was expecting.

"It might have." I never realized that breathing could be so loud. I opened my eyes and Diver was standing directly in front of me, her head to one side, a frown drawing her forehead together.

"Quit playing games with me," she demanded. "This is serious. I've got better things to do than to make a new needle."

"Stand back, then," I told her, and when she did I tried again.

In my head, I drew a picture of a needle and stared at it. Then I threw the needle out into the forest and tried to watch where it landed. Unfortunately, the minute it left my mind, it disappeared, just like Diver's needle had done.

"Well?" She was beginning to be annoyed with me. "Come on, where is it?"

"Tell her," Three Chances urged. "Then she'll leave us alone."

"I can't do it by myself," I said. "I don't know enough about . . . the problem."

"Who can tell you?" Three Chances inquired.

"Only Diver. It's her needle, after all, and she knows more about it than anyone else."

"If I knew that much about it," Diver said, "I wouldn't be here asking a little boy to help me."

Little boy. That stung, just as she meant for it to.

"Tell me about this hiding needle," I asked her, pretending not to have noticed what she just called me. "What sort of a needle is it?"

"It's . . . a needle." Diver was losing confidence in my abilities.

"I mean, is it a happy needle? A stubborn needle? A sneaky needle?" I didn't know what I was asking exactly.

"It's a *lost* needle."

"Yes, yes. I know. But what kind of a lost needle?"

"It's . . ." She struggled to understand what I needed to know. "It's a . . . *sticky* needle."

"You mean at its point?"

"At its point, but also there's this part along the side that keeps snagging on things when I try to sew. It sort of makes a rip in the hole."

"That's because you didn't shape it very well," Three Chances suggested. "You didn't take enough time."

"I was too busy digging cooking stones for you," Diver shot back at him.

"You never take your time," he accused.

"You're always somewhere else when it's your turn to work."

"Wait a minute," I said. "Tell me more about the sticky part."

"You know how a piece of bone sometimes is hard to polish?" Diver asked. "How it's rough and no matter how hard you try to smooth it, it just won't agree with you."

"Especially if you rush," Three Chances broke in.

I stopped Diver before she could answer him. "So,

has it ever stuck on anything besides deer hide?"

"My finger," she said. "Look." She showed me a scab on the inside of her thumb.

I was getting to know this needle a little better. "Anyplace else?"

She thought about the question. "Once," she said, "when I was sewing very late in the afternoon—the sun had almost disappeared—that needle hid from me by grabbing on to my own dress. I didn't find it until the middle of the night when I turned over and it poked me."

This information gave me an idea. I shut my eyes again—I was taking a chance, but I had no other choice. Again I pictured the needle. I pictured Diver using it by the side of the pond. I pictured her deciding to go swimming.

"When you went into the water," I asked her, "did you wear your dress?"

"That's none of your business!" She thought I wanted to know more than was proper for me to know. Maybe she was right. Before I could stop myself, I pictured Diver without her dress—but then I closed the eye that peeped at her and went back to the needle.

"When you took off your dress, where did you put it?" I leaped over the question.

"On top of the shirt I was sewing," she answered before she realized that she had admitted she had taken off her dress. The eye that I had shut flew open and I caught a splash in the water, the bottoms of Diver's bare feet.

"Did you fold your dress or just throw it down?"

"The bugs were terrible. I dropped it."

Again I tried to picture what had happened. I saw the dress fall on the shirt. I saw it stay there until Diver emerged from the water.

"How long did you swim?"

"No time at all," she said. "I heard someone coming so I got right out and snatched up my dress and pulled it over my head."

It was hard to keep one eye in my mind wide open and the other one firmly closed, but I did. I saw Diver's hand reach quickly for her dress, press it down before she picked it up.

"Look at the place where your skirt ends," I told her. "Feel it with your fingers."

"You must think I'm stupid to play your nosy boy game," she said, but still she slid her hand along the fringe at the bottom of her dress. "I'm going to tell my mother that you asked all these questions about my clothes, Walnut. She will speak to your mother and . . . ouch!"

I held my breath until she spoke again.

"How did you do that?" Now she sounded pleased, even friendly.

"You *can* find things with your eyes closed." Three Chances was impressed.

"Not by myself," I said. "I can only see what is put

19

in front of me, like anyone else."

But Diver didn't hear me. She was already running off, excited to have news to tell. By the next day everyone believed I could live up to my name. The truly bad thing was, I began to believe it, too.

CHAPTER 3

OVERNIGHT I WENT FROM being myself to being a person who was expected to know things. I could feel people watching me, their glances like high soft grass I walked through. I couldn't be sure, but I thought they were talking about me as well, about my special sight that was better than ordinary eyes, about how amazingly I had identified Gray Fire and how quickly I had found Diver's needle. I noticed a difference in the way I was treated—how when I visited my relatives I was served my food immediately after the old ones, how uncles and aunts hurried to make room for me in the eating circle, how older cousins didn't laugh anymore when I greeted them by the wrong names until they got closer to me or when I stumbled on a log or bumped into a yard pole.

I liked these differences very much. Soon they no

longer surprised me. A little while after that, I began
to expect them.

"Sees Behind Trees," my mother called to me one
morning when I failed to come outside for breakfast.
"It's time to get up."

"I'm not ready yet," I said. "I'm thinking with my
eyes closed." A cool breeze sifted through the places
where the wood of the house walls did not meet, and
I was too comfortable to move.

"It's corn cakes," my father invited me. "Warm
from the hearth. And then I need you to help me
patch the roof."

"Save at least two of them for me." I tried to speak
without rousing myself, to murmur from some place
other than from my body. "For when I'm finished
thinking."

There was a long time of quiet then, and I imagined that my family was whispering so that they
would not distract me from whatever important
thing I was doing. I let my mind wander, drift and
sail like an orange maple leaf through the blue air.
Every part of my body fit perfectly against the mat I
was lying upon, my legs and arms and head and back
all equally heavy and pleasantly balanced. I let my
hidden eyes look where they wanted, which was
nowhere. Water. I sensed water, sniffed at its un-
mistakable odor—a dry pale wetness. I ran my
tongue along the surface of my lips, straining
toward the beginnings of being thirsty. The water

pooled in the cup of palms, swirled gently over rocks in the creek, glided in long drips down the side of smooth bark.

Poured on my face!

I sat up coughing and rubbing my eyes, spitting and shaking my head.

"Think about that." Brings the Deer laughed. He knelt beside me, to the place he must have silently crept, holding a bowl that was now empty.

"That was not funny," I said very loud. My uncle had always been kind to me, a better friend than any boy my own age, and for him to play some mean joke, just when I was so happy with myself at last, seemed not fair, worse than if someone else had done the same thing. For the first time in my life I was angry with Brings the Deer, confused by him, shocked to be mistrustful of him.

The smile fell from his lips at my tone, but he didn't move except to sit next to me. He touched my wrist lightly with his fingers.

"It will be funny," he said. "When you think of it the right way."

"How can the same thing be both funny and not funny?"

"You have to see the joke," Brings the Deer explained. "You have to learn to laugh at yourself."

"Will you laugh if I dump water on you when you're asleep tonight?"

He thought about my question. "I doubt it," he said

finally. "But in any case I would probably get up and throw you into the pond."

"Because you're bigger than I am. Stronger." The unfairness!

"It has nothing to do with size. At night I have a right to be sleeping. But if you choose to sleep when you should be awake . . . funny things can happen to you." The pressure of his fingers became more insistent on my skin, as if his hand were asking mine to understand what he meant. "Come on outside, now, nephew. There's nothing to keep you from the day. After all, your face is already washed."

All that morning I felt unsure about myself as I worked beside my father repairing the hole in the roof where the rain had found an entrance. The sun was hot on my back and small insects buzzed about my ears. The cloudy autumn sky was a constant white that stretched off forever, and I had to bend close to tie the bunches of dry yellow grass that I then tucked tightly into the rotted-out space. It seemed such an ordinary job to be doing after suddenly becoming grown up, such an everyday task, such a waste of my time.

"Do you remember what happens to the skin of your fingers after you've been swimming in the pond too long?" my father asked from below as he handed up more grass.

Swimming in a cool pond sounded like a very good idea.

"Kind of scrunched together," I answered. "Puckered like grapes that are too ripe."

"Right. Well, that's how your face looks today. Surely Brings the Deer didn't have *that* much water in his little bowl."

I raised my hand to my forehead, and it was true— it was pulled into lines of shallow wrinkles. My lips were as pursed as a clam that doesn't want to open. My neck was stiff and my shoulders hunched high like the wings of a sleeping bat.

"Every day can't be unusual," my father said gently. "Otherwise something wonderful wouldn't mean so much when it happened."

I thought about his words, and my body began to relax.

"But I thought everything was supposed to change when I grew up," I said.

"It does," my father assured me. "And yet it doesn't."

"How can both of those things be true?"

"You're still fixing the roof," my father pointed out. "Just as you did last year and the year before that. Your weight is still light enough to allow you to be on top of our house without falling through."

"So it's all just as it was." Why had I always been told that getting a new name was so important? Why had I worried about it so much?

"Not quite," my father said. He reached up and squeezed my bare foot. "The difference is, now you and I are having a conversation between men."

What he said was so simple, and yet it startled me more than a crash of thunder. My father and I: we were both *men*. A shiver ran like a laugh through my back.

"You mean you're talking to me the same way you would talk to Brings the Deer?" I asked, not quite believing this to be possible.

"Certainly not," my father replied, but before I could be disappointed, he continued. "Brings the Deer is my brother-in-law and I like him very much. But you, Sees Behind Trees, you are my son."

I had never quite understood the dividing line between not being grown up and being grown up. It seemed as though there was some invisible doorway a person walked through and when he came out on the other side he was supposed to be all that he had been before, except more. Yes, I was still my father's son. Yes, I was still Brings the Deer's nephew. Yes, I had learned how to do something new—to see with my ears and to back up what I heard with questions that might help me see more sharply—but I was no smarter than I had been. I was not ready to be a warrior or a hunter, to be a husband or a father. I didn't know how to build a house or sing the late-night songs. I didn't know how to be quiet when it made no sense to speak or to speak when everyone else was silent. I didn't know how to find the special herbs and plants that made medicine, didn't know how to talk to other grown-up people in ways that were both respectful and equal. No matter what anyone else thought—no matter how often Diver repeated her story, no matter how much my mother and the rest of my family bragged about me—I knew who I wasn't: I wasn't who they thought I was. I was still just me, with a different name.

How did other people do it? Had it been easier for them to catch up to their new selves? Or was everyone secretly two people at the same time, one of them largely pretend? I tried to think of the most completely grown-up person I knew, and Gray Fire—the man I had heard in the woods—came to my mind. He had a calmness, as if he lived in a place that didn't require any neighbors. Of course he was polite, but there was still a distance about him. He seemed content with himself, with making his pictures on bark, stringing his shells, doing his quillwork. Though the weroance was his sister and though neither of them had ever married or had children, you never saw them joking or heard them laughing together. I didn't even know if they ate their meals from the same bowl. Was needing to be with no one else what it meant to be grown up?

If that was true, I had received my name too soon—because I hated to be alone and avoided it whenever possible. I slept curled next to whichever brother I could find and all night we would roll and switch positions on the mat, kicking or punching each other, getting close for warmth on cold evenings and waking each other if we had an interesting or scary dream. During the day I was always doing some work for my mother or father or following after Brings the Deer or running off in the afternoons with boys my age to swim or make secret pathways in the high grass. When I was little I hated the game we sometimes played—the one where a person had to close his eyes and everyone else hid away. When my turn came I always looked around and saw . . . nothing, nothing but the closest trees or cornfields or the blur of distant houses. I ran in circles, calling, pleading, until finally every other player gave up and came out. When someone else had to search, I made sure—by not hiding well—that I was the first one to be found. At least that game was different now. Ever since my mother had taught me about seeing with my ears I could find every other player, usually without moving from where I stood. They never let me be it anymore.

Sometimes, now that I was supposed to be grown up, I made a test for myself. I would sneak off, leap into the pond so that my ears were blocked by water, hold my breath, and float facedown. But as soon as I thought: This is what it's like to be alone, I scrambled for the surface, threw myself on the bank, rubbed my hands among the pebbles, and wondered loudly where everyone had gone. Without somebody to watch me, laugh at my jokes, tell me what to do, ask me questions, race me to the river, make me guess the names of birds, or challenge me to count the silvery fish in a school, there was nothing for me to do. Without somebody to be somebody to, it was as though I wasn't somebody myself.

"You only feel that way because your eyes are weak," Three Chances decided when at last I confessed my problem to him.

"They are not weak," I protested. *Try seeing behind a tree*, I wanted to dare him.

"What I mean is," he continued as if he hadn't heard me, "you get alone faster than other people."

He could tell that I didn't understand, so he tried again.

"Your alone space is smaller." He held out both his arms and turned around in a circle. "Anything beyond that and to your eyes it might as well not be there."

"But . . . ," I started to say. *How did he know this about me?*

"Me, on the other hand," Three Chances went on. "I can see as far as I can throw a rock. And *that* far away there are bound to be people, so I'm never alone like you are."

"You really can see as far as you can throw a rock?" This sounded impossible to me, yet Three Chances claimed it so calmly that I couldn't help but take him seriously.

"Well, in daylight, anyway," he said. "At night . . .

at night the rock would probably hit somebody and I'd get in trouble."

Now Three Chances was making sense to me, because at night, with the sounds of sleeping and whispering, the vibration of bat wings swooping in the air, and the low crackles of dying fires on every side of me, I didn't feel so much by myself. At night *I* could see as far as I could throw a rock.

"How far *can* you throw a rock?" I asked Three Chances, wondering which one of us was stronger.

"*You'll* never know," he laughed, making fun of me.

"Well, I know where your foot is," I said, and stamped on it.

"Ouch," Three Chances shouted. "You better watch out, Sees Behind Trees. Some night when you don't expect it I'm going to sneak up on you and make you sorry."

"Just try it," I said, thankful that he had said "night."

CHAPTER 4

THE NEXT DAY I decided to go searching for this new self of mine, and the first place to look was to see if people I didn't know very well had begun to treat me less like a child than they used to. I heard a cluster of men talking together, went to stand just outside their group, and waited for someone to congratulate me— or at least to recognize me or include me in the conversation. I put an expression on my face that said I was interested in what they were discussing, though it was all complaints about their various sisters-in-law and mothers-in-law and I didn't understand most of what their problems were. No matter how much I laughed when they laughed or shook my head when the man next to me shook his head, nobody seemed to notice I was there, so finally I moved on.

Next I heard the weroance herself. She was giving advice to a hunter who was having no luck. I listened as

31

she explained to him about reading tracks, about thinking like the animal he was pursuing, about apologizing many times for having to take its life. The man finally nodded and moved on.

"Hello, Sees Behind Trees," the weroance greeted me. Spoken in her everyday village voice my name didn't seem so impressive—but still, she remembered it.

"Hello," I said back, and then stopped myself. There are different ways to say "hello." You say it one way to your friends, another to your parents and relatives. You say "hello" to a person you don't know with a certain kind of stiffness and "hello" to someone who's powerful in a respectful tone. I didn't know if I had said the right "hello" just now and felt embarrassed. The weroance, however, did not seem to be offended. Instead, she actually seemed curious about what I wanted.

What did I want?

"I just thought," I said, still not quite sure if I was addressing her properly. "I just wondered if there was anything you needed for me to find?"

"To find?"

"You know, you said that sometimes you needed someone to do impossible things. . . ."

She held her mouth very still, but her shoulders seemed to grow, as if she was holding her breath inside herself.

"What impossible thing did you have in mind?" she asked.

I felt foolish to have repeated the words she had used when she gave me my name. In my mouth they sounded like boasting, and I had nothing to boast about.

"I've got to go someplace now," I said, and excused myself quickly.

I walked through the village, not even speaking to people I passed because I knew if I did I would say another stupid thing. Finally, at the very edge of the woods I practically crashed into Gray Fire, who was lounging in front of his small house, peeling bark from saplings. I heard the scrape of his shell knife against the wood before I saw who was making the noise, and stopped myself just in time.

"So, you've found me again," Gray Fire joked. "It seems there's no hiding from you, even in the deepest forest. Here." He patted the ground. "Sit down and tell me how you did that trick. It would be a useful talent for a man like me to know. Maybe then I could predict when my sister was coming and could manage to look busy by the time she arrived!"

Would Gray Fire have said such a thing to me before I became a man? No! He was known to be very quiet, even among the other older men. I joined him, curious to see what would come next.

"It wasn't a trick, exactly," I told him.

"What was it, then? Did you notice that I was not among the crowd watching the contests and guess where I was?"

33

"No. I can never see who's there and who's not in a group of people unless I'm standing directly in front of them or unless they're talking and I recognize their voices."

"But I wasn't talking."

"In a way, you were. I mean, your body was. You limp. When you walk one foot falls heavier than the other. With most people it's just boom-boom-boom-boom. With you it's BOOM-boom-BOOM-boom."

Gray Fire shifted his weight but didn't say anything for a moment. Finally, he spoke.

"I thought no one noticed," he said. "I thought I had disguised that problem, was cured of it." His tone sounded . . . what? Flustered, as though he was admitting something shameful.

"I'm sure no one else pays attention to it," I assured him. "It's just that I have to listen very closely so that . . ."—now it was my turn to reveal an unpleasant secret—"so that people won't realize that I can't see as far as they seem to be able to."

"I've heard that about you," Gray Fire said. "Eyes like a possum."

I hung my head. "I guess I didn't fool anyone."

"I guess I didn't, either." Gray Fire began to work the stick again, each stroke long and even. "But at least *your* problem isn't your fault."

Gray Fire was an important man, an elder, the weroance's brother, a famous artist. I couldn't be so nosy as to simply ask him what he meant, though I wondered very hard how his limp had happened to him. I teased a tangle out of my hair, wishing he would tell me. The lull of the afternoon was striped with the rhythm of Gray Fire's knife.

"So this is how it happened," he said finally, and opened his hands upon his knees to release the story.

"I was young," Gray Fire said. "Not much older than you. And I was the fastest runner in the village."

"You?" I repeated before I could stop myself. I could imagine many things about Gray Fire but "fast" was not one of them.

"It was my pride. Speed." Warmth seemed to come from where Gray Fire sat, as if the morning sun had returned just to shine on him. He leaned forward and in the sparkle of his voice I heard him as he had once known himself. Quick as a water bug.

"Did you win races?" I asked, caught up in his memory.

"Every one. I won so many races that no one would race me. They held special contests in which I was forbidden to compete. They made me the judge."

Our eyes met and I felt a push of excitement, as though I could feel his legs beneath me.

"A *judge?* When you were my age?"

Gray Fire blinked, slowly and deliberately. No words were necessary.

"What happened?"

He looked beyond me, off into the distance. "It's a

mistake to let any one thing about yourself become that important," he said. "It can be dangerous."

"How?" I thought about Brings the Deer and the bowl of water.

"It can make you forget your weaknesses," Gray Fire said. "It can make you believe what other people say about you or need from you more than what you know to be the truth. You start to make promises you can't keep."

Now I was the one who looked away. What if Diver's needle hadn't stuck to her dress? "All right," I finally admitted. "It *was* a kind of trick, seeing you coming. But I don't know how I did it. I mean, I couldn't really see you but I . . . I put together the parts of sounds I could hear and you were the only one I knew that they would all fit."

"Oh, that's good," he said. "That's a very intelligent trick."

I could use the word "trick" for what I had done but I didn't like it when Gray Fire echoed me so easily.

"Was your running fast a trick?" I asked him.

He thought for a moment.

"A very intelligent *skill*," he corrected himself. "I hope you have use of it longer than I did of mine."

My back was becoming tired but I didn't want to complain because then Gray Fire would start to talk about backs or stiffness or how a person had to forget about small problems—and what I wanted him to do was tell me his story. So I pretended to scratch my neck and shifted my weight.

"Getting tired of sitting, are you?" Gray Fire observed. "Well, I could tell you stories about having to be still . . ."

We both waited to see if he would do so.

". . . but I'll save them for another day. You must be patient."

"I'll try," I said. *I'm trying*, I thought.

"Where was I?" Gray Fire wondered aloud.

"You were the fastest boy in the village," I reminded him.

"More than just the other boys. The fastest person." I nodded.

"But not as fast as I thought," Gray Fire explained. "That's what got me into trouble."

Would he ever get to the story? "What did?" I asked. "What got you in trouble?"

Gray Fire drew in a slow breath, let it out. "I thought I could run faster than night," he whispered.

"I believed that I could go as far away as I wanted," Gray Fire continued after a thoughtful pause. "To as strange and distant a place as I could find, and that I could still get back safely before it got dark."

"And could you?" I was caught up with the idea. That would be wonderful, to go anywhere and yet return home when you needed.

"No," Gray Fire said. "There are some places that are too beautiful. You want to be part of them. They trap your heart."

"Where?" To be part of a place, within it, like a purple flower in a summer meadow, like a grain of sand enclosed by a smoky tan agate. A place where you wouldn't have to see to be. I listened with every skill I had learned—because wherever it was, that was where I wanted to go.

"I can't tell you exactly. It was an early afternoon many years ago. I had been on a hunting trip with my sister and we became separated—that's when I discovered it. Without any plan as to where I was going, I stumbled out of the woods and down a winding, steep path into a land of water."

There was amazement in Gray Fire's voice, as if he were in that place again, just as he had seen it the first time.

"Water?" I prompted him to go on.

"Everywhere I looked," Gray Fire said. "Water pouring down from streams in every direction into one great river that led into a lake so wide and long I couldn't see the end of it. I think it stretched all the way to the sea. Where the water met rocks, mist rose to greet the rain that was falling. And the sky, the sky was like the surface of a still pond and reflected back everything that was below."

I tried to imagine such a scene. "What did it sound like?"

"Like a storm," Gray Fire said. "Like the tide turned into wind. Or like the sizzle and snap of a great fire.

Like all the noises you've ever heard, except louder and squeezed together. And I was in the middle."

I could almost hear the place. I noticed that Gray Fire had closed his eyes tightly to see it.

"And the colors," Gray Fire went on. "It was as though someone had thrown a rock into a rainbow and all the pieces were broken up and mixed together, brighter than ever before. Standing there was something like staring into the face of the sun without having to quickly look away. And the longer I remained watching, the more the shades changed. The sky dimmed yet the colors seemed to become lighter."

"Go on," I begged him when he paused. People never talked so clearly about what they saw. Listening to him was like smelling hot soup on a cold evening.

"It was like being in a dream," Gray Fire said. "As the hours passed, I knew I should return to the woods, find my sister."

"You must have wanted to show her that place," I suggested.

Gray Fire brought his large hands up to his face, pressed his fingers against his cheeks. "That's the shameful thing," he said at last. "I didn't want anyone else to know about it. I wanted it all for myself. In fact, you are the first person I have ever told."

"Me?" I was shocked. "Why me?"

Gray Fire held up his hand. "Hear the story first.

"As I was saying," he continued, "the land of water only became more wonderful as the sun traveled to the west. My feet were heavy with wanting to stay. I envied the trees, rooted there, belonging there. Compared to what lay before me everything else I had ever seen was made of dust. Where does a runner run when he has arrived at the only finish line he doesn't want to cross?"

This was a question for which I had no answer. To not want more, to be so satisfied that you didn't want to move, didn't want to be surprised at what happened next, didn't want to hear a new story, learn a new song, wish a new wish, didn't want *more*—to me, that was like being a rock or a stick frozen in the ice of a pond: awful.

"I think I understand what you mean about a place being 'too beautiful,'" I said.

Gray Fire laughed softly to himself. "Nothing is more dangerous," he agreed. "Night was coming quickly and I realized that I should try to find my sister. I knew that, but I told myself that at the last minute I could race the night and win."

"What stopped you?"

Gray Fire put his hand upon my shoulder. His skin was as dry and feathery as an abandoned wasps' nest, but there was a bony strength in his fingers that pulled me into his memory. "The moon. Suddenly the sky above me cleared and the largest moon I have ever seen looked down. Against the blackness of the sky it was the color of a robin's breast. And then I looked down, following its light to the pool where the water was most calm. The moon floated there, too. And it shone also in the mist of the air—each drop contained a tiny orange moon."

Can words show you something you have never seen? Listening to Gray Fire was like watching him take a stick of charcoal and draw a picture on a flat piece of limestone. With each stroke the image became more clear, more complete. I was afraid if I said the wrong thing Gray Fire might stop talking and this vision of sights I had only pretended to know about would blow away. The moon. When people described it they always said it was as round as the dark circle of a person's eye, but to me, even at its brightest, the moon was just a white smear in the night sky. Everything that was far away from where I stood was either invisible or blended together like many shades of clay, like the swirl of leaves that still remain high on the branches of a maple tree at this time of year. Once they fell to the ground and were close enough for me to touch I could tell the differences between them, divide them into orange and purple and red and yellow. Maybe the moon was like that, too—a thing you could understand, once you were near enough.

"The moon on the pool was so huge," Gray Fire went on, "that it seemed to be right in front of me—the entrance to an enormous cave of light. It glittered like flint and I wanted to see what lay within. I took a step, another, to the end of the path. My feet sunk in cold water, then my legs. Before I paid much attention the stream was about my waist and it was pushing at me and holding me at the same time. But I was almost there. I reached out my arm, put my hand through the moon."

I nodded. It was just as I had suspected! Shapes changed close up, tightened into themselves.

As he spoke, Gray Fire slowly lifted his other arm, stretched his hand forward, then suddenly spread his fingers wide and shook them, breaking the sunshine into flashing patterns. "The moon shattered into waves," he said. "I had come too near. And before it could return, the clouds so crowded the sky that I could not even see stars. The rain returned as well. The night had beaten me before I had taken my first running step. And that was not the worst thing."

"Was it the cold?" I asked.

Gray Fire looked at me. "My foot had slipped between two curved rocks," he said. "It had been swallowed by the spirit of the place."

I felt a chill as if an icy wind had blown through my body. I drew my cloak closer around my shoulders. "What did you do?"

"Though I pulled as hard as I could, though I ducked underwater, used my hands, pushed and twisted until I felt the skin of my ankle tear, I could not get free. My two smallest toes were wedged in too tightly. And then the water rose as if a tide were rolling in from the sea. It lapped against my knees, it washed onto my stomach, it passed my ribs. When it reached my shoulders, I realized that I had no choice."

"No choice about what?"

Gray Fire's fingers gripped my shoulder like the claws of a bird preparing to fly. "When I was about to give up, to give in, I heard my sister, Otter, call to me from very far away," Gray Fire said. "She sounded irritated, annoyed that I had disappeared. But soon her cries became so unhappy, so full of grief that I knew I couldn't remain there, couldn't leave her alone. I slipped the bone knife from my belt. I held my breath and ducked underwater. With one hand I steadied my pinned leg. With the other, I cut off my toes that were pinned."

In shock, my eyes darted to Gray Fire's feet, crossed beneath his knees. It occurred to me that I had never seen him without his moccasins.

"The pain was terrible," he said in a distant, high voice. "Even the coldness of the water did not help. I cried out, used all my weight as leverage, and the rocks released me. I backed into the darkness, felt the mud harden as the water became more shallow. I must have pulled myself up on the bank, still wailing, then half scrambled, half dragged myself back into the woods. I must have left a trail of blood, but the rain washed it away—I myself tried to search for it in daylight. Finally I collapsed, slept where I dropped, my head full of water and moons and colors. The next thing I knew Otter was beside me, wrapping my damaged foot in a poultice made of leaves.

"'I searched for you all night,' my sister scolded as

she worked over me. 'Didn't you hear me call? I must have passed near this place a hundred times.'

"'I was somewhere else,' Otter says I told her. 'I was inside of beauty.'

"'Don't talk nonsense. Where could you go? What animal attacked you?' She thought I was confused by my wound and so didn't take my answer seriously. She never has.

"I didn't explain to her, or to anyone. Yet since that night my every limping step has reminded me that I want to go back and look for what I left in the land of water."

"For your missing toes," I said in sympathy.

Gray Fire shook his head. Now his fingers pinched like two halves of a clamshell, then released me.

"For my heart."

We sat for a moment without words. A wind rustled the dry leaves that still remained attached to the branches of the tree behind Gray Fire's house and some of them wafted down, brushing upon the mats of his roof. The air smelled damp, frosty, cold against my cheek. I tried to think of a secret story of mine that I could tell to Gray Fire, something to balance the value of what he had shared with me, but nothing I had done seemed important enough, mysterious enough, interesting enough.

"That's good." Gray Fire nodded in approval. "You understand about listening. You are not afraid of quiet."

"Have you gone back? Is it still as beautiful?"

"I dream of it every night," Gray Fire said. "It's the only dream I have. I've tried to find my way there, tried and tried. I've crisscrossed the woods, attempted to make again the mistakes I made when I became lost that first time. In my wanderings I've seen many odd things—birds with huge beaks, a cave that glows—but . . ."

"But never the land of water?"

Gray Fire hung his head. "I know it can't be far. It took us only two days to return to the village once Otter rescued me. But ever since then . . ." He paused, waited for the right words. When he spoke again there was sorrow in his tone, a hush. "It's as though it has disappeared into my memory."

Gray Fire seemed to turn in on himself, to journey to a place I couldn't follow, so I pressed my fists together and said the polite thing, the words my parents had taught me to use on such an occasion.

"Thank you for the gift of your story."

Gray Fire shook his head, sat up straighter, tapped one long bony finger on the ground between us, and drew a circle in the dirt.

"It is not a gift," he said. "It is an invitation."

"For what? Why?"

"To join me. Because . . ." Gray Fire rested his hands back on his knees. "Because you are Sees Behind Trees."

"Me? You mean I could come with you? Leave

the village? You'd take me to that secret place, just the two of us . . . men?" I couldn't move I was so excited at the idea.

"No."

I knew it was too good to be possible.

"You will take *me*. Perhaps with your . . . skill, you can find the land of water."

"I don't think so," I said uncertainly. If I was lucky, with my skill I could hear footsteps coming, I could guess where to look for a sticky needle, but what Gray Fire was asking was too much. I was not ready. Not quite.

"Say yes," Gray Fire urged. "Say yes." No one had ever made a request to me with such need in his voice. It made me feel scared and important at the same time. *Sometimes*, the weroance had said when she gave me my name, *the people need someone to do the impossible. . . . Someone with the ability to see what can't be seen.*

I stared at the circle Gray Fire had made. The moon, he said, was just as round. I opened my fist, knelt forward, and pressed my palm into the center, leaving the print of my hand like a promise in the soft earth.

"I'll try."

CHAPTER 5

I WAS NEARLY ASLEEP in my house that night when I heard voices outside mention my name.

"Do you know where Gray Fire is taking Sees Behind Trees?" my mother whispered.

"I know where he *wants* to go." I recognized the weroance's voice. She sounded uncomfortable, as if she didn't really wish to talk.

"What do you mean, Otter?" my mother asked.

"It's a place he dreams about," the weroance answered. "He's tried to find it many times but with no success. This won't be any different." She did not sound convinced.

"Is it dangerous? Should I worry?"

"Gray Fire knows the forest better than anyone. He'll teach Sees Behind Trees a great deal. Nothing bad will happen. Gray Fire always returns eventually from these wanderings, tired and disappointed, but no worse than that."

"Have others accompanied him before?"

There was a brief silence.

"No," the weroance admitted. "Sees Behind Trees will be the first."

Neither of them spoke for such a long space that I almost drifted into sleep again, but then the weroance said something that made me completely alert.

"If I could stop my brother, I would. But I think he has waited for this long enough. It is his time to go and . . ." Her words seemed forced from her, like the meat of corn squeezed out of one kernel after another. "This time I must allow him."

"But what about Walnut—I mean, Sees Behind Trees? There's more to this than you're telling me, Otter." My mother was alarmed. I could see her face in my mind—her eyebrows drawn together, her eyes glistening, her lips drawn back across her teeth.

"What will happen to Sees Behind Trees will be up to him," the weroance answered. "As it is, finally, for each of us."

"Where is Gray Fire taking you?" Brings the Deer and I stood together in front of my house in the crisp early morning light. He was annoyed—and something more.

"I promised him I wouldn't tell." I pulled a deerskin robe closer around my chest. The air smelled of winter—sharp and silver.

"But I'm your uncle. I could join you. Gray Fire is a hard man to know and this would be a good chance for me. There's much I could learn from him. Besides, he's old to make a difficult trip as cold weather approaches. What would you do if he got sick or hurt himself?" Brings the Deer inclined himself toward me and showed me the expression on his face. It reminded me of a look I had seen before, but only on very young children who did not want to sleep.

I drew lines with my moccasin in the soft cold ashes of last night's cooking fire. I had never before been in the situation where Brings the Deer wanted something from me, and I was embarrassed that I could not grant his request.

"I'm sorry," I said.

He stepped back, made a noise of irritation. "Why did he choose you?" he asked, but he meant, *Why not me?*

"It's just that . . ." There was nothing I could explain without revealing Gray Fire's private story. "It's just that Gray Fire wants to figure out how I heard him walking in the woods. He said it was a useful skill."

"Then he should ask your mother," Brings the Deer replied. But I could sense that he didn't feel as badly now that he had a reason to rest upon that had nothing to do with some failure of his own. After a moment, while we both watched our breath make clouds in the air, he turned back into his normal self.

"How long do you think you'll be gone?"

"Maybe . . ." I remembered that Gray Fire had said

the journey home from the land of water had taken two days, but of course we had to find it first. "Maybe five days?"

"Then you must prepare yourself," Brings the Deer said. He ducked into the house and I could hear him talking softly to my father, who was of two minds about my leaving: worried that I was too young, and proud that his son had been selected to accompany such an important man on a long trip. Their muted voices sounded like bubbles of steam on the surface of a boiling pot.

In a moment they both joined me outside. Brings the Deer draped his new cape, woven tightly from reeds, around my shoulders. My father placed a small bundle into my hands, then kept his own large hands around mine while he spoke to me. "You may need food," he said. "This time of year you never know what to expect. I packed some flints, a shell knife, a strong coiled rope of grapevine." He hesitated. "Ashes from the cooking fire," he added gruffly. "To remind you where you live."

His hands were gentle, warm in the cold air. They trembled slightly before he let me go. "This is a great honor," he said, and then added, "I will fast until you return home."

By the time I got to Gray Fire's house it had begun to snow. The flakes struck my skin like a swarm of gnats, and when I reached to touch my hair I found my head covered with a crusty cap that cracked and broke apart at my brushing. Surely, I told myself nervously, Gray Fire will want to wait for a better day.

But, no. He was impatient to start out. "It is too early for real snow," he stated. "This won't last. It will melt in no time and by this evening the earth will be brown again."

Gray Fire was not a tall man—and he was slightly bent with age—so he and I were nearly the same height. He was as old as a grandfather but his mind seemed younger—more curious and less sure. His oiled black hair was streaked with white, and his face was brown and round as a chestnut. He clutched his rabbit cloak together with a hand shaped by hard work—knobby fingers scarred by the blades of many hunting knives, nails cracked, wrinkles that slid over muscle and bone. He smelled of smoke and venison and damp fur, and when he smiled to encourage me, many teeth were missing from their places. He— *he*—had picked me out from all the others. There was nowhere I wouldn't go with him.

"How will we find it?" I asked as we passed through the wall of black trees at the back of the village. "What should I do?"

"First," Gray Fire said, "I'll bring you to the closest spot I remember. And then you'll listen and see what you hear."

Once we were in the room of the forest, I forgot

about snow. There was very little wind and the trees acted as a roof to protect us. The floor was gentle with leaves and dry pine. We traveled swiftly and without further conversation. Every now and then Gray Fire would hesitate, press his palm against the flat of a rock, or study a pattern of bark before turning right or left.

"Will you show me how to do that?" I asked him. "How to find your way around out here?" I put my hand on a tree trunk he had just touched. It was soft and mossy.

"Your body will remember where it has been if you let it," he answered. "It recalls what's familiar—but not as your mind does. With your mind you stand outside the world and look in. With your body you are inside already."

I didn't know what he was talking about but I nodded anyway.

"Do you understand?" Gray Fire asked.

"No," I told him honestly.

"Then don't nod your head," he advised. "If you don't admit your confusion you'll never learn anything that you don't already know." Gray Fire balanced his words by raising his eyebrows and pursing his lips, as though he were the one receiving an unwelcome criticism, not me. "Let me try again, because this is easier than it sounds. When rain falls into a river, how does it know which way to flow? When a mouse leaves its hole, how does it ever get back? When a bird flies away for the winter, how does it locate its nest when it returns in the spring?"

"They're smart?" I tried.

"Smarter than you?" Gray Fire inquired.

I thought of a mouse. I thought of a bird. I thought of a drop of rain. "No," I said.

"Yes they are!" exclaimed Gray Fire, and poked at my ribs with his pointy finger. "Because they know not to *think*! If a mouse ever began to consider its situation it would be very unhappy!"

"Why?" I tried to imagine a thoughtful mouse. Gray Fire was right—it did not look happy.

"All right," Gray Fire continued, and stuck his face close to mine. "I am a mouse." Somehow his eyes sparkled, his nose became longer, his arms shorter. He drew his chin into his neck and glanced around in every direction.

I couldn't help laughing aloud.

"What is that noise? What is that awful noise?" Gray Fire cried in a mouse voice. "It was like thunder but smaller. Help! I must run, but where? I am so little and everything else is so big! What should I do? I don't know!"

All the while he was being a mouse Gray Fire hopped up and down in worry.

"Be a bird now," I begged him.

Gray Fire's body changed. He stuck out his neck, inspected the ground with one eye, extended his arms to either side.

"Oh yes, here I am high in the sky," he chirped. "Nothing but clouds below me. Let me think, let me think, where did I leave my eggs? Was it in that tree? Or that tree? Or was it that tree over there? I'm concentrating but . . . they all look the same to me! I'm lost! And when the winter comes, which direction do I fly? Where do I go?"

With that he flapped his arms desperately and opened and closed his mouth.

It was so amazing to see such a dignified man behave like one of my friends, though Gray Fire was funnier than anybody my age. As a matter of fact, he *seemed* like someone my age—as if he had never become completely grown-up. "Now rain," I pleaded, trying to hold in my laughter.

"Your turn." He folded his arms and watched me.

"I don't know how."

"Yes you do."

Rain. I put arms close to the side of my body and turned myself into a straight line. I shut my eyes and pictured myself narrow as a stem.

"I like to fall," I sang, surprising myself, and clicked my tongue. "It's . . ." Suddenly I *was* rain. I remembered what it felt like to leap from the high rocks that overhung the lake north of the village, to sail so fast through the air that once you pushed off there was no more chance to be scared, to have nothing but wind touch your body until the shock of cold water. There was no time to it, no this then this then this—just that thrill of no control, of passing through the world fast, loving the fear, loving the not knowing, loving that you were daring enough to have jumped in the first place.

I opened my eyes and Gray Fire was watching me, smiling.

"Very good," he complimented me. "Now be a raindrop that thinks."

I thought about thinking, and immediately I became worried.

"Oh, no!" I cried. "I'm falling! Catch me! It's so far!" When I wasn't inside a raindrop—when I stood outside myself and thought of all the terrible things that could happen—everything changed.

I shut my eyes and yelled. When I stopped the forest was very quiet. The only sound was the whispering swish of distant snow.

After a moment, Gray Fire spoke. "Now," he said in his regular voice. "Now you can nod."

"I'd still get lost if I tried to go home by myself," I said as I followed him deeper and deeper into the woods.

"You can't get lost from yourself," Gray Fire said. "After all, you're always where you are."

I wanted to object but could find nothing wrong with his statement.

"Where are you now, for instance?" he asked me.

"Here," I said.

"So. You're not lost."

"But I don't know where 'here' is."

"Look around you. This is where 'here' is."

"You're playing word games with me," I complained. "You act as though you don't understand what I mean, but I'm sure you do. I may be 'here' but if I want to go 'there' I wouldn't be able to find it." I thought Gray Fire was making fun of me, so I didn't stop myself from saying a hurtful thing. "Just as," I added, "you can't even find your way back to your water place."

Gray Fire stopped walking and turned toward me. "You're right," he said sadly. "'Here' is both places for me. Perhaps I've wanted 'there' too much. A person must let his destination pull him. It's like with relatives: it's one thing if you demand to own something that belongs to them. It's another if they choose to give you the same thing as a gift. The object is not important. The act of giving is what matters."

I felt so bad that I had been disrespectful to Gray Fire that I hung my head and told him a secret I had never admitted to anyone else.

"What I want too much," I said, "is for my eyes to see the way other people's see, if only just once."

"I understand, grandson," he answered softly. "But remember what I told you about not letting a thing be too important. The truth of it is, you already see better."

CHAPTER 6

GRAY FIRE HAD BEEN wrong about the snow. It didn't
stop, and as the afternoon grew darker the whiteness
lining the lower boughs of trees thickened. In clear-
ings where no branches separated the sky from the
earth, the air before me was flooded with flickering
motion and the ground was smoothed with drifts fine
as salt. We had barely paused all day and I was not
cold, but thin layers of ice coated every puddle.
Snowfalls like this were rare, especially early in the
autumn, and I knew my father and mother would be
worried about me, even though I was with a man so
experienced. Still, I hesitated to ask Gray Fire about
returning home. Every step we took away from the
village was a step nearer to where he wished to be,
and it was not for me to judge when far was too far.
I watched to see if he slowed down or became tired,
but just the opposite seemed to be happening. As

57

Gray Fire led me along the trail of his remembering his limp seemed to improve, as though drawing closer to his missing toes improved his damaged foot.

Once this idea occurred to me I stayed at Gray Fire's side so that I could watch his feet—and I had a surprise. Not only was his limp much better, but when he walked he made almost no tracks in the snow. The first time I noticed this I thought I was simply not seeing well, so I stooped to feel for the impression of his moccasin in the fresh snow. There was but the barest hint—just a greater firmness where he had passed than in the surrounding path. Every little while I would pretend to scratch my ankle and check again, and if anything his footprints became even fainter. He passed over the powdery surface like a gust of wind. Compared to him, I was the heaviest and clumsiest moose. Every place we went I left the deep marks of my presence, but the snow kept no record that Gray Fire had gone before me.

At last we paused under the shelter of a rock ledge. I opened my bundle and offered Gray Fire some dried venison that my mother had pounded with blackberries, but he shook his head.

"I eat very little," he said. "But you go ahead."

I bit off, chewed, and swallowed the first pull, but it was odd to eat alone—I found I wasn't as hungry. "Tell me about how the weroance saved you?" Again I offered Gray Fire some of my jerky and again he shook his head. "You said the two of you were hunting?"

When Diver had requested that I find her needle, asking questions had helped me—maybe they would this time also.

"I opened my eyes and the first person I saw was my sister," Gray Fire said. "That was of course before she became weroance."

"She was a good hunter, even then?"

"The best." Gray Fire's voice smiled. "As I told you, I was a runner but Otter was—still is—an expert tracker. She's never returned to the village without success. From earliest childhood, she was clever and quick."

The weroance I knew was heavy and slow moving. Her voice rumbled like stones tumbling down a hillside. But once, I realized in a flash, she had actually been a girl just as now I was a boy.

"What was she like? Otter?" I felt daring to use the weroance's name, but Gray Fire didn't seem to mind.

"She would not be denied," Gray Fire said. "She had to be right, always—and the strange thing is, she was."

I shrank the weroance in my mind, made her slim and determined but not yet in charge of everyone else.

"If she said it would rain, it had to rain," Gray Fire recalled. "And it did. If she wanted a fish for supper, someone would catch it no matter what the season. If she woke up early to see the sunrise, everyone else had to come outside and admire it with her. We are twins, you know. But she was born first and I never

59

caught up. I believed everything she told me."

"Like what?"

"That I was fast—and I was fast! That I should come hunting with her—and I went. It was she who taught me how to shoot a bow."

"*She* threw the moss into the air? Not your mother?"

"As I said, Otter could not be denied. I think somehow she knew she would never have a child of her own and so she became my second mother."

"And your first mother didn't mind?" I couldn't imagine my own mother letting anyone else take her place with me.

"I wonder," Gray Fire said. "She must have. But I don't remember that she objected. Otter had a way of making you believe that you wanted what she wanted. Being right mattered so much to her that those few times she made a mistake, no one could stand to see her disappointed. We were . . ." Gray Fire hesitated as if searching for the exact words. "We were shielding her from discouragement," he finally said.

"So, when you wanted to stay longer in the land of water and you heard her call? . . ."

"I had to leave." Gray Fire rubbed his hand across his chin. "I had to," he repeated, as though he were talking to himself.

"Do you remember cutting off your toes?" Ever since Gray Fire had told me his story I had tried to

imagine myself doing such a thing. It was impossible!
Even considering the notion now, when I was used to
the idea, made my feet tingle.

"It's strange," Gray Fire said, "but I don't. When I
dream of how exactly I escaped the land of water,
there is a blankness. One moment I am fixed in that
place and the next I am waking up beneath the boughs
of a spruce tree."

"And there she is," I interrupted. "Otter."

"And there she is," he agreed. "Frowning. Worried.
Bandaging my foot and blaming herself for allowing
me to become separated from her."

"And you didn't tell her where you'd been?"

Gray Fire did not like my question. "I told you
before. I was selfish about my discovery. I am ashamed
to say that I kept it to myself. And now we should stop
talking. Use your skill."

The ledge above us magnified the rustle of the forest, making it more difficult for me to search for what
was not ordinary. It was like sucking water through
my teeth—anything that was thick stuck on the outside. And there, what was that? People, I was sure of
it. A man and a woman, arguing with each other. As I
ignored every other sound their conversation became
on the one hand more distinct and on the other hand
even less clear. Even though I could hear two voices I
couldn't make out what was being said.

"We aren't alone here," I told Gray Fire. "But I can't
tell who is nearby."

"Which way?" he asked quietly, turning his head from right to left. "How many?"

"Two," I answered. "Over there." And pointed to my left.

"How far?"

"Just beyond those trees. They don't know we're here, at least I don't think so." It was startling to hear people talk but to make no sense out of the sounds. Had I become so mixed up that I had forgotten how to understand words?

"Perhaps they know where the land of water is," Gray Fire whispered. "Perhaps that's why they're here, too!" In a low crouch he headed off in the direction I had pointed.

I was right behind him, trying to match his quiet steps so that we would not be overheard. As we approached, the voices became louder but still they made no sense to me. Soon we reached a dense cluster of pine and stopped. The speakers were just on the other side, still tossing slurred sounds—perhaps they were not even words—back and forth.

I squinted through an opening in the needles and indeed there were a man and a woman seated by a low shelter made of leaned-together birch poles. They were stretching a large bearskin on a frame made of bent branches, tying it off to dry with sinew strings. As I stared, the woman, without looking, reached back and felt for an awl. Her face was practically right before mine. She was neither young nor old, very thin. Her eyes drooped slightly on the outside. Her nose had been broken and had healed sideways so that it seemed to be pointing to her ear. As she stretched, dimples appeared in her cheeks. She was not an unpleasant looking person, and yet I had to control the urge to shout in fright. Because here's the incredible thing: I didn't know who she was—and I knew everyone!

I turned toward Gray Fire. There had to be some explanation. He shook his head very slightly, indicating that I should remain calm. I looked through the pines again and this time concentrated on the man. His outline against the forest background was large and round, suggesting great weight. His hair was long and worn loose around his big shoulders. His lips, when I squinted very hard, were as red as if he had been eating wild strawberries. I couldn't believe it! I didn't know him, either!

Gray Fire pointed to a tree behind us and then led the way. I could hardly stop myself from asking questions until we were far enough away not to be overheard. The moment Gray Fire stopped I gripped his arm.

"Who are they?"

"Strangers," he replied. I had heard that word used before but like many grown-up expressions it didn't mean anything special to me. I thought strangers were some kind of make-believe beings, like the talking animals parents told their children about or the creature who was supposed to be half fish and half human.

"*Strangers* are real?" Even the sound was lumpy on my tongue, as if I had tasted food that was not properly cooked.

"Oh, yes. They are *like* us, but they are *not* us," Gray Fire answered in a distracted tone.

Not. Us. Excitement and fear ran a race around my mind, first one ahead and then the other catching up and passing. When they were both out of breath, I was able to talk again.

"Do you mean," I asked, thinking very hard, "that . . . that . . ." The idea was almost too big to carry. It changed everything. "Do you mean that there are *people* besides us? Actual *people*?" Suddenly I didn't know anything for certain. Suddenly anything was possible.

"Not exactly," Gray Fire answered. "As I said, they are and they aren't."

"Like ghosts?" I suggested.

"No," Gray Fire said. "Ghosts are people like us, only changed in their form. They were our relatives— somebody's aunt or someone else's grandfather. When they visit our dreams or thoughts they always have some purpose, some job for us to perform. We know what they want: respect. We know what upsets them: being forgotten or laughed about. Ghosts, compared to strangers, are not difficult."

I glanced back in the direction of the voices, which

continued to scratch at my ears.

"What makes strangers difficult?"

"Not all of them are difficult. Some can be interesting or funny, though even the best of them are in some ways ignorant as babies. They can't talk sense or understand it. They behave rudely, laugh at the wrong times. They are secretive and unpredictable, eat odd foods, dress in unusual clothes—or no clothes at all! And sometimes they even seem afraid of us."

"Afraid of *us*?" Another new idea!

"Yes! They act suspicious, are always looking behind themselves. And the bad ones . . . well, they are worse than weasels."

"What do they do?"

"They steal." Gray Fire used another one of those words that meant little to me, and frowned. He could see my confusion, so explained further. "They have been known to snatch objects that they didn't make, even when someone else needs them. Once, I've heard, they even took one of us."

"Took? Took one of us where?"

"Away, to wherever they go. They took my great-uncle when he was still a little boy. People never saw him again. His name was Acorn."

"Why did they take Acorn?"

"I have no idea," Gray Fire admitted. "It was long before I was born. Maybe they were lonesome, but that's no excuse."

What, I worried, if these ones on the other side of

the pine trees decided to take me? Fear passed excitement and ran fast down a hill.

"But most strangers are not dangerous," Gray Fire added, as if hearing my worry. "Just confused and usually hungry. Sometimes they even have good things to trade—black fire stones, beautiful shells, furs. After they learn to talk they can tell stories of their adventures and of places where they have been but we have not."

"The bearskin," I said, thinking out loud. And then, "The land of water."

Gray Fire nodded. "We must greet them," he said. "Just in case. And besides, meeting strangers is an adventure for you, news to report when you get home."

Unless they take me!

"Let's go." Gray Fire stood up, brushed himself off. "Make a lot of noise so they will hear us coming and not be surprised. Remember, to them *we* are the strangers."

We! But before I could explore this amazing idea Gray Fire was halfway to the clearing and I had to hurry to catch up.

"HERE WE ARE, OUT FOR A WALK," Gray Fire shouted. "WE ARE PEACEFUL PEOPLE. WE HAVE NO WEAPONS. WE ARE FRIENDLY."

"Can they understand you?" I whispered.

"I DON'T KNOW IF THEY CAN UNDER-

STAND ME BUT I HOPE SO," Gray Fire continued. "IF THEY CAN THEN THEY WILL NOT TRY TO KNOCK US DOWN."

As if in reply, the voices in front of us got louder. "DRAK BETAK LAK LAK," yelled the man.

"LAP DUWAP AGGAK NU," yelled the woman.

"I think they hear us," Gray Fire said, and ducked through the low branches.

The man and woman, one round, the other narrow, were standing in front of their shelter. When they saw us they became nervous, bending at their waists and making motions with their hands and the same barking noises with their mouths. They *did* seem afraid—but it was only us!

"Lak lak," the man repeated and pointed to a basket of dried meat near the fire. "Lak lak."

"Thank you," said Gray Fire. "I'm sure it's delicious."

"Can you understand what he's saying?" I asked.

"I hope so," Gray Fire answered, and reached down to take a piece of jerky. The man clapped his hands to encourage us.

"Aggak nu," the woman said, and pointed to a steaming pot. Even from where I stood I could smell it was some kind of tea.

"Yum yum," Gray Fire exclaimed, as if he were addressing a small child. He even rubbed his stomach.

"What's going on?" I whispered.

"Dinner," he answered. "I think."

➔   ➔

Soon we were seated on mats set in a small circle, each of us with a bark bowl of tea. When Gray Fire finished, he looked at the woman. "Aggak?" he asked.

"Aggak!" she nodded, and scooped more into his bowl.

"Now we're getting somewhere," Gray Fire said to me. He pointed to the smoke rising out of the pot, and then to himself. "Gray Fire," he pronounced slowly.

The man and woman looked blankly at him and then at each other. They made some sounds between themselves and then both turned their attention back to us.

"Gray Fire," Gray Fire repeated, pointing first to the steam and then to himself.

At first the woman made to offer him more tea but stopped when he said his name a third time.

"Grape Wire," she said haltingly and brushed her hand from the steam toward Gray Fire.

It was Gray Fire's turn to nod. "Yes," he said, and touched his chest. "That's me. Gray Fire."

"Ah," said the woman, and spoke quickly to the man. "Ah," he said, then pointed to Gray Fire. "Grape Wire?"

"Grape Wire!" Gray Fire smiled and touched his chest again. Next, he pointed to me, then cupped his ear with his palm, then pointed to me again: "Sees Behind Trees," he said.

The man and the woman understood instantly.

"Sees Tees," they both cried, and patted my shoulders. His hands were plump, hers as firm as sticks. "Sees Tees."

"Now you," Gray Fire suggested, and gestured toward the man, whose face glowed with figuring out the game. He searched on the ground until he found what he wanted, then held up a red pebble with one hand and tapped his forehead with the other.

"Karna," the heavy man said clearly. His shoulders and arms were thick with muscles and his neck was wide as his head.

Gray Fire and I looked at each other.

"Karna," the man tried again.

"Karna," Gray Fire and I said at the same time, and the man's smile got wider.

"Pitew," the woman announced in a high, reedy voice.

"Pitew," we answered in the same tone.

Now at least we knew who we all were. Or so I thought. Pitew and Karna spoke quickly back and forth to each other, all the while glancing at us, then finally seemed to decide something.

"Checha," they agreed together. Pitew walked quickly behind their shelter. I heard her rustling through a pile of leaves, making humming and chirping sounds, and when she returned she was holding a bundle of fur to which a few goldenrod stalks still clung.

"They have a baby," said Gray Fire, and I scooted

closer to see. And sure enough, peeking out of its warm covers was a round, serious, sleeping face. Its pink lips were parted, its dark lashes were long and thick, and its eyebrows were arched in such a way that I was sure it was having a good dream.

"Checha," Pitew said, this time to us, and held the baby up for us to admire.

I was used to holding my younger brothers and sisters and so did not hesitate to take the baby in my arms. It stirred, as if realizing that something was different, and opened one eye to study me gravely. Pitew hovered close by, ready to take the baby back if it became frightened.

"Checha," I said softly, which seemed to satisfy it— I couldn't tell if it was a boy or girl.

I brought the baby over for Gray Fire to see.

He looked briefly, then smiled at Pitew and Karna. "Handsome," he said.

"Do you want to hold it?" I asked.

He shook his head so slightly that no one but I could notice.

"It's my sadness," he said, "and my sister's, that neither of us ever married, never had sons or daughters. It was a promise we made to each other after my accident. That day—it set us apart from the usual flow of life, froze us together as we were, as we had always been. Otter said that the whole village would be our children." Gray Fire sighed. I had the sense that he had told these words to himself many times before and never quite been consoled by them. After a moment, he spoke again. "I would be awkward holding a child but I don't wish to insult our hosts."

The baby awoke again, struggled an arm outside its wrappings, and reached its hand toward my nose. As I rearranged the furs I took the opportunity to discover that he was a boy. A hungry boy, I realized, as he began to kick and fuss. I gave him back to his mother who adjusted her robe and put him to her breast. All the while, though, I was thinking about Gray Fire. Holding a baby was the first thing—besides not being able to find the land of water—that he couldn't seem to do.

As the afternoon wore on, Gray Fire had no luck in explaining the land of water to Karna and Pitew, though he tried. He squeezed snow in his hand until a few drops dripped from his fist onto the ground. "Water," he told them. "Land."

But Pitew only showed her teeth in a smile and Karna imitated Gray Fire and made a snowball of his own. Of course, we were no better in understanding what they were trying to tell us. It had something to do with the country to the south, something about warning us. They would point to themselves, then in the direction birds fly in autumn, then shake their heads and make alarmed, fearful faces.

"Maybe there are bad strangers there," I suggested.

"It's possible," Gray Fire agreed.

"Are there lots of bad strangers?" I imagined bunches of them waiting everywhere, and all I wanted was to be back with my mother and father, safe in the house, still a little boy who wasn't expected to know anything—like Checha, who was asleep again, in the cradle of Karna's folded knees.

Karna and Pitew, fortunately, were the best strangers I could hope for. They kept offering us more food and insisted, when the light disappeared, that we sleep next to them near their fire. Every now and then one of them would say something and the other would chuckle as if it were the funniest joke they ever heard.

"Why do they laugh all the time?" I asked Gray Fire.

"The same reason we do," he answered. "They are relieved. We are no trouble."

As soon as he spoke I realized that Gray Fire and I had been chuckling a lot also. Not ordinary laughs, but ha-ha-ha-aren't-we-having-a-good-time laughs that took the place of words. Sometimes Gray Fire and I and Karna and Pitew did nothing but look at one another and laugh reassuringly. Sometimes even Checha seemed to laugh, too, joining in.

"*Ha ha ha,*" Pitew might begin.

"*Ha ha,*" I would answer.

"*Hee hee hee hee,*" Karna would add.

"*Ha ha!*" Gray Fire would say, and it somehow felt as though we had shared a conversation, though no specific information was passed around. There was another thing about this way of speaking: trying so hard to be friendly made me very tired. Halfway through one of our laugh-talks I closed my eyes. The last sound I heard was Pitew's increasingly faint *"Heh . . . heh . . . heh."*

I woke in the early dawn light with the sound of . . . nothing . . . in my ears. Ever since I had received my new name I had begun my day with listening, with waiting for the world to announce itself. Today, only leaves and a thin cloak separated my head from the earth and so I sorted out the pulse and rumbles of the ground, the partings of stiff grass, the melting of snow. It was a language more familiar to me than the one spoken by the strangers, and it told its own wordless story. Deep within its memory I heard the passage of steps taken long ago, of seasons pressed upon its surface, of plants digging their way into the air. I felt the flat-pounded earth float like a boat on still waters, like a butterfly that pauses in its flight as steady as if it's perched upon a slender branch. I sensed the chill of winter covering summer like the first ice crust that layers a pond.

Opening my eyes, but otherwise not moving, I watched Pitew, Karna, and Checha in sleep. The mother and father curled beside each other close as two ash trees with tangled roots. Her hand rested on his mountain of a chest. A strand of his fine black hair had floated across her brow. And between them, like a nest fit securely in sheltering branches, lay Checha. He rested on his back with his arms stretched out on either side, connecting the three of them.

Gray Fire slept with his head on his bent arm. With each breath a pale frosted puff rose from his mouth and mixed with the day. It was a trick of the light, or perhaps just my eyes again, but his skin seemed almost to shimmer as though it were the reflection of itself in a pool of water.

Water. Reclosing my eyes and blocking out all other sounds I searched for the place that Gray Fire remembered. I was sure it flickered just beyond my reach the way the cries of birds sometimes blow past in breezes. But where? In which direction? Was I imagining the land of water because I wanted it to be there for Gray Fire, or was it real?

Wait. There was a call. A sparkle of light danced among all the other sounds. It was so clear that it blended with the noises surrounding it—I had been hearing *through* it instead of hearing it, but once I found it there was no mistake. Such music could only come from one place—though it was gentler than Gray Fire had described—and that place was not far away. It had been close by all along.

CHAPTER 7

I KNELT BY GRAY FIRE and whispered in his ear, "I found it."

He sat up so quickly that our heads knocked together, and when we both rubbed our hurt spots and said, "*Ow ow ow,*" Karna and Pitew opened their eyes and looked at us.

"*Ow ow ow,*" they each mimicked, and rubbed their own heads, as if they believed that this was the polite way to say "Good morning." Checha, who was unusually watchful for a baby, simply looked confused.

Gray Fire attempted to smile but I had the feeling there were no more laughs inside him—he had used them all up last night.

"What did you say?" he asked me.

"I found it," I repeated. "The land of water. Now that I've learned how to listen for it, I can hear it plainly."

"Even now?" His eyes were afraid to hope.

"Even now."

Gray Fire got to his feet, straightened his clothes, and dug into his pack until he found a small bundle of wrapped leaves tied with vines. He held it out to Pitew, nodding for her to accept it. "Thank you for sharing the night," he said.

Pitew looked doubtful but still she unwrapped the bundle. Inside were shelled walnuts, brown and sweet, but she seemed not to know what to do with them. Gray Fire made eating signals with his hands and mouth and finally Karna was curious enough to try a bite. You could tell that he was the kind of man who rarely refused food. He picked a small nut, stared at it closely before putting it into his mouth, and then crunched down with his teeth. He looked surprised at the taste, then chewed again. This time he was happy and took a handful more. Watching him, Pitew also bit into a walnut, then held it for a moment while she decided what she thought.

"Wal-nut." Gray Fire gave them the name. "Good."

"Goot?" said Karna uncertainly. "Ah, *goot!*" He held up the last one before popping it into his mouth. He chewed and chewed and then, when the walnut had been turned to mush, he took some out and fed it to Checha, who licked his lips.

"Goot," agreed Pitew.

It would take too long to explain that they had chosen the wrong word, so we didn't bother to try.

→   ←

Once we left the camp and went back into the forest, the land of water proved harder to locate than I had expected. No matter how much we walked, it always sounded to be the same distance from us, and by midday—the hour of no shadows—Gray Fire had become impatient.

"We are traveling in circles," he complained. He sounded weary and discouraged—and I was afraid he was right.

"I don't understand why you can't find it," I answered peevishly. "You said that a person's body remembers where it has been."

"You don't learn a trail that you've only run upon in pain," Gray Fire said, shaming me. But then, as he had done before, he took away the sting. "I depend on you, Sees Behind Trees. I am sorry that I questioned your skill."

Still, every once in a while Gray Fire would point out something—a tree or a boulder—that he said we had passed before, but the circles we made must have been bigger and bigger because the familiar landmarks were, each time we came upon them, farther toward the center the second time we found them. It was like following the path of a whirlpool, except instead of spiraling into the middle we were carried further toward the outside shore.

Since Gray Fire had given away his food and insisted that I save for the trip back the provisions

77

Brings the Deer had given me, we were both hungry, and I began to worry that we were lost. Yet . . . there it was again, that music, drawing me, promising just a little more walking. The water pounding a drum with an uneven beat, a familiar rhythm but one I couldn't place until I realized that it matched the song of Gray Fire's limp. With every step, all these years, he had been dancing to its call.

"Stop," I told Gray Fire. "Stand perfectly still."

And in the silence, the uneven echo of his footsteps beckoned me toward the dimming light, across the untrampled snow, through a low, narrow tunnel in a high wall of rock all but hidden by a dense stand of fir trees, on the underground path to the land of water.

"We're here," Gray Fire whispered as he emerged behind me and stood up. "It is just as I remembered."

"What is it like?" I asked him, and closed my eyes to see better what he would tell me. "Describe it to me."

"I don't need to," he said. "This place is different. Open your eyes."

A moment ago the dark shapes of trees were close about us and now we were out of them. The earth had turned from the soft mat of leaves to the sleek cold smoothness of wet rock. The ground dropped away—we were standing on the rim of a cliff of some kind. The space before me had the feeling of a huge cave. I was inside a rain cloud, my hair heavy on my head with moisture. My clothes hung lank on my body. Large drops rolled down my cheeks and neck and arms, down my forehead into my eyes. At first I wiped them away, but they only returned in greater number. The water was soothing, warmer than the air, clean as tears. In its embrace I lifted my chin, inhaled a long filling breath. Blinked.

And saw.

The shock of sure sight was so great that it didn't surprise me. There were so many things, rows and rows of them stretching into the distance! Objects I had always studied one at a time now crowded together: trees and rocks, water and land. I couldn't move, I was as still as Gray Fire must have been when his foot got stuck, but it seemed as though I was spinning very fast—seeing made me dizzy. There was so much to know, to drink in! Trees had tops! The water had a far bank! Clouds! *That's* how they were shaped: white with *edges*! I could see in flashes every bit as far as I could throw a rock. Farther. As the rain splashed my staring eyes my vision sharpened and diminished, and with each coming and going a burst of pure clearness appeared before me. The blue scene fit together like jagged pieces of a hatched robin's egg. I sensed Gray Fire still at my side but I paid no attention. All I could do was look and look and look.

The view was as he had said that day in front of his house: beautiful. In the river, white water swirled and whirled around dark stones, and where the two crashed together a fine watery dust filled the thick air like pale dandelion seeds. Fine snow mixed with rain and glittered where it landed on patches of ice. Water poured and blew and rushed and laughed, and I raised my arms toward it, spread my fingers wide to catch it, tasted its sting on my tongue. I had never been anywhere so completely. I barely noticed at first when Gray Fire pushed past me and started climbing down the cliff—except to realize that he looked the same even when the distance between us widened and to be amazed at how steeply the gorge fell. I had never gauged anything so low from anywhere so high.

When all is in movement, you eventually notice the thing that is still. Below me down a steep bank in the shallows was a stark black silhouette the size and shape of a man, half crouching. It must be a young tree—surely those were branches twisting forth from its trunk. The more I stared the more I wasn't certain. Was it a boulder? It could have been my shadow, so exactly did its posture match my own.

In my blinks of focus I could see Gray Fire swiftly approaching it, becoming smaller and smaller, climbing over driftwood, leaping effortlessly from rock to rock. He ran without stumbling, faster than I had ever known a person could go. His streaming hair now seemed all white. His skin and clothes were speckled with snow. Never had he seemed more to be his name, and I leaned forward, called, "Gray Fire," but he couldn't hear me above the din. He flew, he matched the water with his speed, he passed over it like a skipping stone. He got closer to the dark shape and the two of them blurred together, the white with the black. As I strained to see, Gray Fire seemed to sink into its depths like an arrow shot into mud.

I should follow him, I thought. Make certain that he was all right. But then my eyes lifted, swallowed the sights around me. I could see sky. I could see a rainbow arch above the lake. I could see everything I had only guessed about and I didn't want to risk losing this moment by taking a single step away from where I stood. I could stay here forever and it would not be long enough. I could live content in the land of water. I could . . .

Inside my thoughts, in the place where before now all my distant seeing had been done, my mother's face floated like a water lily. My father's hand. Brings the Deer kneeling over me with his dripping bowl. Diver as I had imagined her leaping into the pool. I closed my eyes to see them better—and it was as though the strength had gone out of the wind. The drum ceased to tremble. When I finally looked again, the rain had turned to drizzle and everything farther than my outstretched hand was as it always had been, a blend of wish and doubt.

"Gray Fire," I shouted again. How long had it been since I had called him the last time? In the new stillness my voice bounced back at me, unjoined by any answer. He had slipped—I knew it. He had forgotten that he could no longer run.

I recalled the sight of how sharply the side of the cliff descended and how far it was to the bottom. It was too dangerous, too scary to climb down when I couldn't see where I was going. Even Gray Fire had probably fallen. I couldn't do it.

"Gray Fire," I called again, determined to hear him answer—but there was only the thrash of water beneath me and the silence of the forest behind. If I didn't help Gray Fire, no one would.

If I had been the one lost, he would not leave me.

I stood trembling, stuck in a different way than before, pulled between what I knew I didn't want to do and what I knew I had to do, and then I bent my body. I put my hands flat on the rock and dangled one foot over the side until I found a bush for it to balance on. The other foot reached lower until it met an out-crop of sturdy root. I let go of the rock with one hand and used it to grab the bush's branches. I took a breath, shut my eyes so that I could concentrate completely on what I could feel, and raised my other hand from the edge where I had stood.

"I'm coming," I yelled, my face pressed against the dirt. "I'll find you." Then grip by grip I slowly descended, worked my way down the bank toward the place where he had vanished, the place that now I could imagine but could no longer see.

I don't know how long it took, but it was long. The

light faded. I counted my breaths until the number
became too large and then I started over. My finger-
nails broke, my knees got bruised. Sometimes I had to
use the rope my father had sent with me. The slope
went on and on, each new step a problem I had to
solve, a risk I had to take, a fleeting relief when I
didn't fall backward into the watery air.

Finally, in the darkness of the night, I found myself
on a wide ledge and rested, must have slept. Was it
moonlight that woke me or the faint winter sun? I
couldn't tell the difference, but I started again, pleading with Gray Fire to direct me, listening for the
sound of his breathing, for the limp of his broken foot.

It was brighter when I stumbled over Gray Fire's
deserted moccasins on the last island of rock before
the wild water began. I picked them up, tucked one
under each of my arms so that my hands would still be
free to hold on as I waded in. They were as stiff from
the cold as if they had been set in clay.

The sun was halfway up when, a while later, I
bumped my shoulder against a large stone, big as I
was. It had to be the stone man I had seen from high
above—for "man" was the only way to describe it. No
wood-carver could have done a better job of imitating
a human form. I trailed my hands along the smooth
surface of the boulder, found a nose, twin depressions
that could have been blank eyes, lips parted as if into
a smile, the strong neck, the long line of backbone,
the bent legs that water flowed between, the knees

lapped by curling waves as if the man had been fishing and waited for his net to fill. I reached down to touch the bottom, found the feet where they merged with the rock floor—feet that would never move. My fingers counted the bumps of toes. Five on the left foot. All five on the right.

CHAPTER 8

AN ADVENTURE ALONE IS different than an adventure that is shared. I had journeyed into the woods because of Gray Fire's need. He had determined our destination and I had followed willingly, eagerly, trustingly, never thinking beyond our arrival. Gray Fire was my torch in the night, the hand on my shoulder, the voice that would answer when I asked a question. He knew who I was. His presence was the shelter above my head, the path home. As long as we were together I had in some ways never really left where I started because we carried that place between us like a familiar blanket.

Without him, I expanded in all directions, limitless, thinning, the scent of a rose once it has leapt from the flower where it was born and mixed into the air. Without him I was dispersed, a part of every other thing, purposeless, unanchored. The constant wash of the rushing water stopped my ears and made my shouts no more distinguishable than the slap of the sea or the cries of invisible, angry birds. I could not even hear myself beg, "Come back," to Gray Fire as I clung to the cold skin of the stone man.

But Gray Fire was gone, either drowned or reunited with that part of himself that had never gone from this place. And there was no one to tell me what to do but me.

I loosened the grip of my hands and immediately they began to shake. I was wet and chilled, tired and afraid, as far away as it was possible to be and still be alive.

My mother had taught me how to see inside my mind what I couldn't see with my eyes, but now I taught myself how to hear when my ears were plugged.

"I am Sees Behind Trees," I said to myself without making a sound. "I am a man." And I was. And I was.

That is how I climbed up that icy wall, by giving myself directions, one after another. By allowing my body to retrace the path it had followed.

"Let go," I said, and I let go. "Find the rocks that rise above the water," and sloshing through the shallows, I found them. On the way up I slipped back almost as much as I went forward, but not quite. My arms and legs scraped raw, my head ached, my throat closed in soreness, but each time I paused I was higher than the last time and finally I came to the flatness where I had stood when Gray Fire had sped past. Behind me, below, was the land of water, the only place I had ever really seen and could ever really see, and I knew that if I turned back even once, if I opened my eyes to the rain, I would become like Gray Fire—and never truly leave. In front of me was the blur of green and white that I recognized as the forest. I was balanced once again, pulled both ways, and in that pause—as if between two breaths—I felt Gray Fire's moccasins, still close beneath my arms. I held them in my hands. The heat of my body had made one of them more supple but the other was still stiff as wood. That one I tossed back over my shoulder. The other I threw toward the trees, and when I heard it land I ran toward it.

The forest is large but in some ways it is also small. Any noise that is unusual jumps out, draws attention to itself.

Someone, far away, was crying.

"Who is it?" My voice startled me with its loudness.

The crying stopped, but when I listened more carefully I could almost hear a muffled sigh.

"Karna?" I tried. "Pitew?" Perhaps they had followed us from their camp. I rubbed my eyes to make tears in hopes that would let me see better, but they only blurred my vision further. As I wandered back in what I believed to be the direction we had come, I tripped over roots, stubbed my toes on rocks. My shins and face were scratched by low branches. Finally, lost, I stopped to listen.

So many sounds—drips from melting snow, the chattering of squirrels, the songs of birds. And the smells: rotting logs, summer grass not yet completely dead, mint, and . . . yes, smoke. It could only be from Karna and Pitew's cooking fire and with my eyes barely open I followed its widening trail back from the land of water, away from Gray Fire, toward home.

The smell of burning wood became stronger and stronger, making it easy for me to find my way. It had to come from a large blaze—perhaps they were drying the bear meat, I thought—and the idea reminded me that I was hungry. But when I finally came to the clearing all thought of food fled from my mind.

Karna and Pitew's shelter was black smudge that, as I got closer, turned into a charred mass of birch poles. Swaying in the wind, its moan and sigh were the cries I had heard. After listening very hard and hearing nothing more, I got down on my hands and knees to examine the area, and everywhere I crawled I discovered more destruction: pieces of broken bowls, the shattered frame on which the bearskin had been stretched, the mat upon which we had shared our meal—now torn and ripped. I even found the remains of wrappings of Gray Fire's walnuts. There were many footprints in the slushy snow, many bushes that had been tramped upon, but no people.

"Pitew?" I whispered, suddenly afraid for myself. I rolled under the branches of the pines from which Gray Fire and I had first looked upon the strangers, bunched myself small. "Karna?"

There was no answer, just the overpowering odor of smoke and the hollow sound of emptiness.

"Checha?"

Sometimes even a certain type of silence makes a noise. It gets deeper, more still, makes a hole within the bigger quiet. That's how I knew the baby was still nearby. But where? I tried to remember everything about our first meeting—how after Karna and Pitew had made sure that Gray Fire and I were not danger-ous, Pitew had gone behind their shelter. I heard again the rustle of leaves. Of course! She had hidden the baby. In my mind I saw Karna pointing to the south, making his worried face. Bad strangers.

Staying close to the tree line I worked my way around the clearing until I was behind the smoldering shelter, then I put my ear to the ground and waited. After a little while I heard a sound more regular than any other, the rhythm of breathing. It came from the direction of a bright hill of leaves, raked out from the clearing. I crawled to it on my stomach and gently began to brush it with the tips of my fingers. In no time at all I touched the fur wrappings, and when I peeled back a thin piece of hide, there was Checha, his eyes wide, his lips pressed tightly together, his little body tense.

"Checha," I said in the high, singsong hello voice a person uses with babies. "It's all right."

When he heard me, when he saw it was me, he seemed to let go of all his tightness. As I picked him up, as I held him against my chest and rocked him from side to side, he opened his mouth. And he screamed.

If Gray Fire had still been with me I was sure he would have followed the fresh trail, saved Karna and Pitew from whoever had stolen them away. He would have known exactly what to do, but I didn't. All I could do was comfort Checha and promise him, over and over, "Someday we'll find your mother and father. Someday you'll be with them again. I'll get people to help. Don't cry. Someday, someday."

After a while he seemed to become more calm. The tone of his wailing changed from fright to a sound I was sure I recognized: he was hungry. But how could I feed him? Once again I cast my mind back, recalled the details of our visit only a day before. I saw Karna chew the last walnut, then take the pulp from his own mouth and put it, on the end of his finger, between Checha's lips.

There was still food left in the pack my father and Brings the Deer had given me the morning we had left the village. I bit off a piece of jerky, worked it between my teeth until it was soft as a ripe berry. I spit into my palm and with my other hand scooped a tiny portion on the end of my smallest finger. At first Checha turned his face away, yelled louder. This was not what he wanted, not what he was used to.

"I know," I sang to him. "But it's all there is."

He looked at me, as if trying to decide whether to believe me, then he opened his mouth in a tiny crack.

"Good," I said, and pushed in some meat.

He made a sour face, a pouty face, but after a moment he opened his mouth again, this time a little wider.

"What a smart boy," I complimented him. "What a brave big boy you are. Next time there'll be some corn cake."

And then he smiled.

Gray Fire was no longer with me, but in some ways he was. When I became discouraged, when I lost hope, his words echoed in my memory.

"Your body will remember where it has been if you let it," he had told me. "It recalls what's familiar—but not as your mind does. With your mind you stand outside the world and look in. With your body you are inside already."

I remembered the examples he had given to explain what he meant: rain, a mouse, a bird. At the time it had seemed like a game—funny and silly. But there was nothing funny in being alone, lost in the forest in early winter, with bad strangers around and a baby depending on you. Now I needed to *truly* understand what he had been talking about.

"All right," I said to my body. "I hope you remember better than I do." I had made a sling of my cloak to carry Checha and he rode high between my shoulder blades. At the sound of my voice he reached out a hand to touch my left ear.

"So you think we should go that way?" I asked him.

He made a deep sigh and dropped his head against the back of my neck.

I thought about Gray Fire touching the sides of the trees as we had come through the woods. Why had he done that? Then the idea came to me: moss! It only grew on one side of a tree, didn't it? And I had touched it as we were leaving the village, which meant that as we returned the nearer sides of the trees and rocks should be bare but the farther sides should be mossy. It wasn't a lot to go on, but it was something. I knelt beside the nearest boulder and felt all around it until I found the soft, spongy growth.

"This way," I said to Checha, and looked for the next big tree. It took a long time to pass through the forest in this manner, but at least I knew we were headed the right direction. And every few steps I would stop, stand perfectly still, and listen for any sound that would call me—or make me run away.

That first night I made a fire with my flints and we slept sitting under an old cypress tree. We didn't lack for food, since Brings the Deer had been generous, and there were still a few berries that had dried on their stems and shone through the snow. The weather had turned warmer, and when I looked up, milky starlight showed in patches through gaps in the heavy boughs. Halfway through the next day my feet announced to me that we were crossing a path whose grass had been beaten down by many moccasins. It had to lead somewhere, but should I take it right or left? Once again I searched for a patch of moss, and followed its trail.

Checha was such a quiet baby, absorbed in his own thoughts and dreams. I spoke to him, explaining my decisions, and the sound of my voice seemed to reassure him, to lure him into contentment. What danger had taught him this silence? I wondered. Whatever it was, whatever Karna and Pitew had done to show him how to become still as an animal that seeks to be invisible, it had saved him. Just as finding him, I now believed, had given me a reason to save us both.

The second night we stretched out on a large flat rock that extended over a narrow, fast-paced river whose voice I was certain I recognized. I dozed off to the sound of waves and splashes and suddenly, in my dream, I was standing once again in the land of water. And I could see! I could see the sharp line of sky, the curve of stones, the jagged fringe of trees. I could see the moon, as Gray Fire had described it. The sight so amazed and dazzled me that I awoke with my eyes filled with tears, and when I blinked, spreading the moisture over my eyes, for just the flash of an instant I *could* see, I *did* see, the face of the moon, round and glowing, before it faded into dimness.

"Thank you, Gray Fire," I whispered, understanding, at last, why his dreams of the land of water had been so important to him. Except mine were not tied to that place, trapped and left behind as his toes had been. Mine were in my eyes and mine, I now knew, might come true from time to time.

And the next afternoon, still following the path, I reached the pond where Diver had lost her sticky needle. I was home.

CHAPTER 9

JUST AT THE EDGE of the village, I made out a hunched-over shape. As I came closer I saw a broad back wrapped in a cloak of beaver fur. Closer still. The person's face was cupped and hidden in gnarled hands.

"It's Sees Behind Trees," I announced. I unhitched the sleeping Checha from my back, sat at a respectful distance, and held him, still wrapped in his furs, on my lap.

"Who," the person answered, "knows that better than I?"

The hands dropped away and I found myself staring directly into the eyes of . . . Gray Fire! No! Not Gray Fire, but someone so much like him that it had to be . . .

"It was I who gave you that name." The weroance did not sound at all like her usual self. Each word was pulled from her like the groans of river ice when it melts in the spring. The lines of her cheeks were deep as the ravine, and down each one coursed a shining stream of sadness.

"I have something to tell you," I said. "Gray Fire . . ." How could I explain how I had lost him? "We found the land of water. I could lead you there . . ."

The weroance made a noise that was like a laugh but had no happiness within it. "I have always known how to get there," she said. "How could I forget it?"

"But why didn't you show Gray Fire, then? He searched and searched for it—for his whole life."

"He could never have found his way back," the weroance said, and inclined her body toward me. Her eyes were sleet. "Without help."

Why was she so angry? Did she blame me for not taking better care of her brother?

"He ran past me," I explained. "Just when I could see."

"*Ran*," she repeated. The word was as tired as if the weroance had just completed a long journey. "He never stopped running in his dreams."

"He told me he used to be fast. When he was young. Before his foot got stuck. He told me the whole story."

The weroance looked at me very closely. "Gray Fire didn't know the whole story. Only I do."

Secrets inside secrets. Was this what being grown up was all about? I rested back on my heels and waited. After a time, the weroance began to talk.

"We are twins, he and I. I was first and pulled Gray Fire behind me into the world. Our eyes were open. We were holding hands so tightly that the midwife had to smear grease on our fingers to release the grip. But even when we were not touching we were never far apart. If I was awake, Gray Fire could not sleep. If he was hungry, I needed our mother's breast more. If he learned the name for something—a bird, a plant—I knew it at the same instant without ever being told. From the beginning, we could talk to each other without using words that anyone else could hear. Our father worried about us—that perhaps we were mute because we never cried, never said 'mama' or 'dada' like other babies. But it was just that we had nothing to say to anyone beyond ourselves and when finally we began to speak it was with full and perfect language, for we had practiced it in our silent conversations.

"Can you imagine what it is like to never, even in sleep, be alone? To always know the comfort and music of another's honest thoughts?

"As we got older, of course, there were differences. I became well known as a hunter—perhaps he told you this? I could picture a deer in my mind and it would appear before me as if answering an urgent call. I could follow tracks on a ground covered with dry leaves. I could catch big fish without using bait.

"Gray Fire could do none of those things but, though we looked so much the same that from a distance or from behind people often confused us, he was the more thoughtful. He was always drawing pictures, always trying to capture the sights he loved. And when he became a young man he could run so fast and so far that I couldn't keep up.

"Most people learn what it's like to be alone by getting used to it gradually in small bites, accustoming themselves as if to the taste of a strange fruit or to the fit of new moccasins. But for me it wasn't that way. The first time that Gray Fire kept going beyond the point I could match his endurance, aloneness dropped over me, wrapped around me, caught me in its gluey web. Half of myself was suddenly gone. I breathed out but I could not draw breath back in. I looked with one eye, heard with one ear. My heart beat only half as often. I was half alive. Less than that. To be one when you have always been two is a deep and narrow pit.

"So I decided to change things back to the way they had been. In my hunting I had stumbled upon this land of water. I realized how my brother would love it, how it would claim him with its colors and clouds. He always wanted to be inside one of the pictures that he drew on slate or formed with designs of porcupine quills on birch bark, to remove the distance of seeing, to be absorbed by sheer beauty, to be whole with it. One day I took him near enough to find the place on his own, then I left him by the entrance to the tunnel, knowing that when he passed through to the other side he would not be able resist exploring what he found there. By dragging branches I had devised a route he would instinctively follow, a snaking trail down the side of the cliff into the depths of water. It called to him the way hunting has ever called to me: with a yearning that cannot be refused."

The weroance had been telling her story in a low voice, looking past me into the open space, but now she put her face beside me, whispered directly in my ear.

"An irresistible trap."

She sat back, went on with the tale. She laid it down flat and ordinary as if she were explaining how to carve a bow or the correct method of planting corn.

"A good hunter knows many ways to snare. The loop of vine pinned down by a bent sapling that will spring back when stepped upon. The platform of heavy logs supported by a branch that, when brushed against, will collapse with crushing force. The trench whose bone-breaking drop is concealed by a fragile roof of twigs and brush. But the most clever trap of all is the one that does not kill, that only holds the prey until the hunter comes to claim the prize."

She paused, made a rope of her hair, and clutched it with both hands. "There is a certain arrangement of stones that allows a foot to enter easily, but not to escape."

She let that image sink into my mind, then continued.

"I planned, of course, to go to Gray Fire's aid. I would hide until he had given up hope, then rescue him—and he would be so grateful that he would never run away from me again. We would never be separated, because for the second time I would pull him free.

"But I made a mistake," she said. "I shouted out his name. I made my voice sad and desperate—a last touch to remind him how much he needed me." She stiffened her neck and pulled her hair taut.

"I had underestimated my brother's love for me. It was greater than for any outer beauty, greater than the pride he took in his swiftness. Like a wolf who would rather bite off his own paw than endure the clamp of a trap, Gray Fire did not wait for me to release him—he came when I called."

The weroance shook loose her hair, bowed her head, then raised her eyes to meet mine.

"After that day, he could no longer run away from me, it's true, but he didn't come back the person he once had been. A part of him, the part, I realized too late, that I loved best, remained in the land of water, waiting, drawing him back each night in his sleep. I knew when you left together that he wouldn't return."

The weroance began to weep, her whole body shuddering with each breath. The day I had received my new name, I had no idea how many trees there were, and how much there was to see behind each of them.

Checcha, awakened by our conversation, began to kick his legs, trying to release himself from his wrappings. The weroance, even in her grief, could not help but notice.

"What have you got there?" she demanded. "A fox? A badger?"

Checcha threw off the furs and waved his freed arms in the air.

"A baby," the weroance and I said at the same time.

"How?" she began. "Who?"

"He's a stranger," I said, and added, "but a good one. A very good one."

The weroance bent close to examine Checcha, and I realized that she was as unused to being around babies as Gray Fire had been.

"Here." I placed Checcha in her arms.

"No," she protested. "Gray Fire and I made a promise not to marry, not to have children. I don't know how to . . ." But Checcha paid no attention. He shifted his body until he was comfortable, then looked at the weroance with his large, dark, curious eyes. She touched his chest, touched each of his hands, each of his feet, each of his toes. Old age fell from her face, just as Gray Fire's running feet had finally left behind his limp.

"He likes you," I said. Then I thought of a better way to say it: "He likes you, Otter."

"Don't be so mysterious and important," Three Chances chided. He wanted to know everything that had happened from the moment Gray Fire and I had left the village and was frustrated when I shook my head.

"Do I have to *guess*? Gray Fire got sick? He went off with these strangers that nobody in the village has been able to find?"

"No," I said, wondering as I wondered so often what had become of Karna and Pitew. "Nothing like that." Brings the Deer had earlier asked me the same kinds of questions and been just as impatient when I couldn't answer. I knew my mother and especially my father were curious also, but they were so happy to have me home—and my father was so glad to be able to eat again—that they could wait until I was ready to talk about my journey. Every time they passed by me they would touch my hair, my arm, my neck, as if to prove to themselves that I was back. Even my brothers and sisters were glad. They argued with one another as to who would share food from a bowl with me, who would sleep next to me on the mat, who would help me find the little things I was still always losing.

Three Chances, however, was insistent.

"All right," he began again. "You and Gray Fire left

the village. It was snowing. You headed south. And the first thing you did was . . ."

He waited, tapping his fingers together to urge me to finish his sentence.

"We ate some dried meat," I offered, but he brushed that aside.

"Get to the exciting parts," he pleaded. "The strangers. Finding the baby. Losing Gray Fire."

"Not yet." I tried to sound regretful, and I was—I didn't want to make Three Chances upset with me. And after a pause, he nodded, just as Brings the Deer had done. It would not be polite to repeatedly ask something a person is not ready to tell. It would embarrass both people involved.

"At least," Three Chances couldn't resist adding, "don't tell anyone else, especially Diver—who I know intends to pester you—before you tell me."

I smiled, glad that there was something I could promise him. "You'll be the first."

The problem is you can't really tell a story that you don't yourself understand. If you admit your confusion people are suspicious that you're holding back something, and if you say more than you're sure of, no one believes you anyway.

The version of my adventure with Gray Fire that I eventually told—first to Three Chances and then to Brings the Deer and my mother and father and Diver and later retold and retold many times—was true. We had gone into the woods together in search of a beautiful place he remembered from long ago. We had met a family of kind strangers. We had found the beautiful place and Gray Fire had not been strong enough to return. But with the help of the stranger's baby—whom people took to calling Acorn because his own name was so odd on their tongues and because they thought of him as the lost one restored—I had seen behind the trees once more and found my way home.

When Checha (my youngest brother now that my mother and father have adopted him) is older I will tell him the *whole* story, even the parts I don't understand. The weroance has named herself his grandmother and promises to teach him every secret she knows about hunting. After he has learned all that—and when he is ready—he and I will go out into the forest together. We will search for Karna, search for Pitew, search until we find them—and make the circle whole.